PINEVILLE TRACE

OR

FRANK, THE MISSING YEARS

A Novella-in-Flash

PINEVILLE TRACE

OR

FRANK, THE MISSING YEARS

A Novella-in-Flash
By Wes Blake

Etchings Press
University of Indianapolis
Indianapolis, Indiana
2024

This publication is made possible by funding provided by the Shaheen College of Arts and Sciences and the Department of English at the University of Indianapolis. Special thanks to the students who judged, edited, designed, and published this novella: Abby Bailey, Liza Harris, Aaliyah Hughes, and Amber Phillips.

UNIVERSITY *of*
INDIANAPOLIS

Published by Etchings Press
1400 E. Hanna Ave.
Indianapolis, Indiana 46227
All rights reserved

etchings.uindy.edu
www.uindy.edu/cas/english

Printed by IngramSpark

Published in the United States of America

ISBN 978-1-955521-34-5
28 27 26 25 24   1 2 3 4 5

Cover image by Erik Rust
Cover design by Abby Bailey

Excerpts from this novella originally appeared, in somewhat different form, as "Pineville State" in *Book of Matches*, Issue 10.

Contents

To Natalie

Part One

Pineville State

He leaned his head against the cool glass bus window and felt the vibrations of movement in his temple. His bright orange jumpsuit reflected in the glass. The light outside was soft and about to leave. He closed his eyes and imagined the town they would be driving past: Pineville. As the bus jerked and rolled down 25 East, he imagined a gray stone house at the edge of town, surrounded by a small sanctuary of pines. Sitting at the top of a hill that climbed toward mountains. Near the top of the ridge. Behind the gray stone house, beyond the crowd of pines that surrounded it, tired winter trees—oaks and sycamores bereaved of leaves and green—leaned and struggled to stand up among the proud evergreen.

He wished he was a pine.

Tiredness pulled at him and tried to drag him down through the bus seat, through the bus floor, and down into the gray highway. But the cold window against his face and the vibrations of the bus inside his temple jolted him away from sleep. The green leather seat felt warm against his legs, and the engine murmured.

He kept on thinking of the gray stone house amid the pines, resting at the top of the hill.

A couple minutes had passed since he'd seen the sign for Pineville. He opened his eyes and saw the sweep of the town ahead, to the right of the road. The town was on a ridge as he'd imagined. On the side of a mountain. Pine Mountain. He looked toward the top of the ridge to see where the gray stone house would be. He imagined it would be near the very peak of the ridge, at the edge of town. He closed his eyes again, and his left temple felt numb from constant contact with the cold glass and vibration that buzzed through it.

He dreamed of a diner at the bottom of the ridge. Near the highway. In town. With cool, clean white tables. And booths. An empty diner. And a waitress with dark hair wearing a black apron wiping a tabletop with a damp, white cloth as the world darkened outside the bright diner's luminous interior.

The waitress walks back into the kitchen. And his dream vision can't see beyond. Maybe she sits on a wooden chair against the wall and smokes a cigarette. Maybe she tucks her straight dark hair behind her ear and exhales a smoke stream. In his dream, he wishes he was the short order cook. Wishes he was washing dishes in the kitchen with her, breathing in the warm comforting bleach scent arising from the hot dishwater—blended with the scent of her cigarette, gripping the steel scrub tight in his hand and scraping against the black iron skillet.

But in his dream, he is trapped outside the kitchen. His view obscured by the realities of a dreamer without a body. Stuck in a booth. A perennial customer. Outsider. Passing through.

A sweeping right turn, and the bus engine accelerating

to climb a hill, brings him away from the diner. Awake again. He sees a black Buick coming toward them in the other lane. His old car. Same year. Same model. He wonders if he has dreamed his whole life.

A yellow sign appears—spotlighted by headlights: "Prison Area: Do Not Pick Up Hitchhikers." He moves his head away from the cold window. His temple and face are numb from cold, and the vibrating continues inside his head. He thumbs the fraying rough cotton of his bright orange jumpsuit sleeve and thinks, "I'll bet I can convince someone to give me a ride."

Pine Mountain Pass

He laid on his back, on top of the thin prison mattress, with his hands behind his head, looking up. His eye trailed a dust mote floating in the blinding morning sunbeam that poured through the window. His eyes squinted against the bright, and he felt warmth on his eyelids and forehead. He imagined Pine Mountain Pass as it used to be. As the final difficult turn in a long journey. He imagined a Shawnee hunter passing through. Going home. Back north. And west. Always west. He couldn't imagine going any direction except west; it would go against every legend and myth that breathed in this slab of time and land that he knew.

At dusk, in the last moments of soft light, he'd look up at the pine-dappled ridge—holding onto the warm last light—and imagine animals and people passing through. Along the path. His mind's eye would see Daniel Boone—the big turtle—walking slowly and surely along the ridge in the dusk. Other nights it was a Shawnee woman, among a group of Shawnee, stepping lightly along the final pass of the path of warriors.

But most of the time he'd stand outside, behind his white cinder-block-walled prison dorm, feeling the dusk-cold enter his fingers and the back of his hands, sick with the pleasant scent of Camel cigarette smoke, and see the ghost of a buffalo—stopping to eat acorns from the ground, moving among a group of buffalo down the path, looking for a good open place to bed down for the night. The ghost buffalo had almost reached the fertile valley. Like Moses she could look out over her promised land. This was her path. Across the mountains. The buffalo created this path. And for generations they walked their path. The trace left by their bodies was clear, wide. The Shawnee followed the buffalos' trace. They were wise and listened to the animals. And followed them. And Daniel Boone listened to the Shawnee.

In the dark after-dusk, Frank's cigarette ember burned red, near the tan butt. He imagined one lone buffalo remaining. Still walking the old path above the ridge. Still following her ancestors' path. He felt something brush against his right calf. He looked down at the long-haired gray cat. She looked up at him and meowed. "Hello, Buffalo," he said. He leaned over and stroked her soft fur, under her ear, and petted her along her back. She stretched her back up to meet his hand. "Are you hungry, sweetheart?" She meowed again. Even in the dark he could see her green eyes looking up at him. He flicked his cigarette out onto the concrete, took a piece of tin foil from his pocket, unwrapped it—revealing the ground hamburger, and set it down on the concrete slab. Buffalo ate the hamburger quickly, purring. He petted her side while she ate.

Buffalo was used to his bleach-scented hands. When he first started the dishwashing job, she sniffed his hand tentatively the first two nights. But now she accepted it as his scent.

The hamburger was gone. And Buffalo licked at the empty tin foil. "How goes your recon? Have you found a clear escape for us?" Frank said. The sound of Buffalo's tongue scraping against tin foil ceased. Crickets chirped. In the woods, an owl called out. Buffalo looked up at Frank and rubbed her side against his left calf. "You already know the way, don't you? Your ancestors knew it, didn't they?"

Buffalo circled his leg, and he petted her side.

"I'll follow you," he said. Frank sat down on the concrete slab that jutted along the back wall of the prison dormitory. He leaned against the cinder block wall and felt the cold press into his back. Buffalo climbed on his lap and laid down. He felt the vibrations of her purring against his leg. He stroked Buffalo behind her ears and looked up at the black pine ridge that blocked out the stars.

KY-190

I'm sitting at my writing desk listening to an audio recording that I made last month while driving on KY-190, through Pine Mountain. On February 8, 2022. I hear myself talking, in a voice edged with tired and manic energy, about the new book I will write about Frank Russet. Frank is the main character from my first novel. I say the first lines of the book will be: "He imagined a town he'd never been to. A town named Pineville. Maybe there was a house on the hill. Around a curving drive. At the top of Cedar Street. Backing up against the ridge." Later in the recording, simply titled "KY-190," I hear myself quote another opening: "I imagine a town full of pines. A town I've never been to. I imagine a house on a hill. Cedar Street. The house backs up against the ridge."

In the recording, I am driving down the winding KY-190. The road weaves and winds through Pine Mountain. The highway is all steep climbs, descents, sharp curves. Towering pines spring up beside the road. It looks like Oregon. So many tall old pines. With broad, stable trunks. When I see them, they make me feel relaxed. My destination is Bell County Forestry Camp. In my novel, Frank Russet—the main character—stayed there after he was sentenced for fraud. I had never been to Bell County Forestry Camp before. I researched the minimum-security prison, learned its history, and looked at satellite images to learn its physical layout. And I imagined the rest.

I made the audio recording on a warm, bright February day. A day not to be expected. I had slept poorly in a hotel the night before. Driving in the day before I had noticed a Bell County Forestry Camp sign. And when the next workday ended I found myself following these signs.

When driving east, before reaching Bell County Forestry Camp, you pass Pineville. The name of the town was what led me to the place. Both in fiction and in real life. I had imagined the house from the first sentence. And I wanted to find a house like it in the real world. I felt it must exist.

So I drove through Pineville, starting in the lowlands by the highway, taking the streets up to the ridge's edge. The edge of Pine Mountain.

***

At the uppermost edge of town, I drive up Cedar Street. I drive along Cedar, up the steep ridge. And follow as it breaks left when the land gets too steep. And I see my house. Just like I imagined. Perfect. Even better than I imagined. "I imagine a town full of pines. A town I've never been to. I imagine a house on a hill. Cedar Street. The house backs up against the ridge."

I wanted to live there. And never leave.

***

When I get close to the entrance of Bell County Forestry Camp, I see a yellow sign at the side of the road that says, "Prison Area: Do Not Pick Up Hitchhikers." Just then, a car passes me on the other side of the yellow lines. It looks like a black '59 Buick LeSabre. Like the car Frank Russet drove in my novel.

The land opens up beside me as if for a lake. I take a left onto the road that leads to Bell County Forestry Camp. A sign tells me that I am trespassing and may be arrested. I consider this. I drive a little further on and turn around, backing off the road onto the brown, leaf-covered ground. Before I turn back on KY-190, I pass a woman in a Range Rover parked by the side of the road. Her window is down, and she is smoking a cigarette.

***

After the recording ends, I write this. It's the first Sunday in March. And out the window I see the raindrops have stopped falling into the small black pools of rain on the blacktop drive. I see Rorschach mold shapes on a pin oak trunk. Across the road a lightning bolt strikes above a crowd of trees. But there are no pines to be seen. My cat, Pig, sits on my desk, looking out the window with me. I had been afraid to listen to the recording. Afraid that the manic weather and poor sleep would make it incoherent. Embarrassing. Repetitive. Meaningless.

***

After I drive past the woman smoking in the Range Rover, at the edge of the forestry camp on Pine Mountain, I think about Frank. Think about his life. And his story. About what it adds up to. What it's about. I say into the recorder: "I always tell the same story. Over and over. It's the story about getting what you want. And the story about not getting what you want. It's the only story I know." A few seconds later, I say, "I've got this truck on my bumper. I can't think clearly."

After I finish writing this, maybe I will lay down. And rest. Or maybe I will read in the beige recliner. I didn't sleep well last night. I should probably rest a while.

Sometimes it's so hard to rest.

Escape

Under heavy moonlight, high on the ridge, Buffalo and Frank walked along Pine Mountain Pass. Moonlight—unblocked by leaves which had long since fallen and yet to spring back—illuminated their path. When they walked beneath crowded pine trees, the path darkened but never so much that they couldn't find their next step.

To their right, a grassy opening led to a rocky overlook. They walked off the path into the clearing to look back down on the place they'd left. Buffalo placed one paw on the cool, moonlit-drenched stone and Frank looked back over the valley at their old home—the prison dormitory and campus lying in the valley. Frank leaned over and stroked Buffalo behind her ear. "Remember Lot's Wife."

Frank stepped back onto the path and Buffalo jaunted ahead, leading the way. Frank guessed no one would notice they were missing until morning. He wore khakis, leather boots, a flannel shirt, and a blue jean jacket he'd bought off a cook. By the time morning came, he hoped to find a road, hitch a ride to the bank—where he'd squirreled away some cash no one knew about—buy a car, and be off.

By dawn Frank felt the cold deep in the bones of his hands and feet. His ears and nose burned red and felt numb. He picked up Buffalo and carried her for a stretch down a steep hill. The dawn dampness was on the ground and would stay until the sun burned it off. Frank held onto branches of small trees with his left hand, while he held Buffalo against his chest with his right arm, and stepped carefully down the muddy, moss-covered path. There will either be a creek or a road at the bottom of this hill, he thought.

He saw light gray. A gravel road.

Down the gravel road, the walking got easier. The morning sun rose over Pine Mountain and had begun to change the thick dew into a hovering fog. Buffalo walked off the path and licked dew from blades of grass, keeping a watchful eye on Frank. He slowed his walk and waited until she joined him again. He knew she would jaunt ahead of him again when she had drunk her fill. Between the ridges a narrow patch of cloudless sky was above them. Frank looked at the dull stars still showing. It had not been a good night for stars; they could not compete with the luminous moon. Frank felt his hands, feet, ears, and nose begin to warm. He felt sunlight against his face.

An engine sounded far behind them. Frank picked up Buffalo and carried her against his right breast. She felt warm against him. After what felt like a long time, the sound was upon them. Frank walked at the side of the road, his left thumb stuck out. All his energy was focused on the vehicle. Before he turned he knew it was an old Ford truck. He turned back toward the truck, looked toward the driver—a middle-aged woman with dark blonde hair—smiled, holding his left thumb out and holding Buffalo against his chest.

***

Frank felt the truck's heater warming the outer layers of his body. Buffalo put her front feet on the windowsill and watched the trees go by. The gravel crunched under the truck tires.

The sun was swimming toward the middle of the blue-sea-sky. The muffled engine sound was comforting. Between the murmur of the old Ford and the heat that unfroze his hands, feet, ears, and nose, Frank felt he could easily drift into sleep. Frank said: "Thanks so much for the ride, ma'am. Me and Buffalo appreciate it. We got lost. If you're going anywhere close to the Middlesboro bank, I can get you some gas money there and call my wife. I'll worry about finding the car later."

The woman nodded. "Sure, I'm going through Magic City." She was short and leaned forward over the wheel. But her body was relaxed and sure.

"We appreciate it." Frank looked out the passenger-side window, in the same direction as Buffalo. The gravel road snaked around the ridge like a river.

They drove on in silence. Frank's body thawed. Slowly. First the outer parts, the extremities—fingers, hands, toes, nose, ears—until his chest and head felt warm like he'd drunk hot coffee. The gravel road turned into a paved one. The ridge became the valley. The woods became the town of Middlesboro.

The old Ford passed under a green traffic light on Main Street in downtown Middlesboro and turned into the bank parking lot.

***

Frank walked out of the bank and picked Buffalo up where he'd left her, near the front door. Through the truck's driver-side window, he handed the woman a five-dollar bill. Frank said: "Thank you."

She nodded again. "Your voice is familiar."

"Yeah? Everybody says I sound like that preacher. On the radio."

"That's it!" She hit the steering wheel with the open palm of her right hand.

"You look like him, too. But older. More tired."

"We all have a twin. Me and Buffalo thank you for the ride. I hope someone will help you if you ever need it." Frank patted the cool side of the truck door with his free hand. He nodded and started to turn away.

"Maybe it will be you."

"Maybe. I always try." Frank paused like he wanted to say more. But he stopped himself. Instead, he gave a close-mouthed smile, turned, and began to walk away. Behind him he heard the murmur of the old truck's engine become distant and gradually disappear.

Salesman

Across the street from the car lot, in a small park with scattered trees and wood picnic tables, Frank had left Buffalo sitting under a large pin oak. He had told her to stay put. Sitting upright like a lion, she had watched him walk away.

He had to look tough. Serious. He considered his khakis, boots, flannel. He wished he had his old suit: pressed black slacks, black suit coat, fine black silk socks, polished black shoes, a bright, starched white button-up shirt, and his silk black tie. In that suit he could convince anyone of anything. Even himself. At least he used to be able to.

He walked across the winter blacktop street, stepped onto the curb of the lot and wondered if he could convince anyone of anything anymore. Thinking like that, how could you fail? Frank shook his head and grinned at his own mind.

After taking a deep breath—his back straight and his shoulders upright but loose—he took on the appearance of confidence and walked across the lot, toward the sales office.

The bell clung against the door behind him. A salesman wearing a wide red tie, sat behind a desk. Frank said: "I know what I want—the closest thing you've got to my old '59 Buick LeSabre. If you give a fair price, I'll pay cash."

"Alright," the salesman said. He stood up behind the desk, awakening to his fresh sale. "We've got your car. Follow me."

Frank followed the salesman out onto the lot. Frank caught the scent of cologne and whiskey. The blacktop was starting to lose some of its night-cold. The salesman led them toward a Chrysler New Yorker. They stopped in front of the shiny black car. Frank and the salesman stood back looking at the black Chrysler shining under the mid-morning sun. "This sounds just like your car. Just came in yesterday. Won't stay long. Car like that wants to move." The salesman patted the car's roof. "Big American car. Practically brand new. Most popular car of '71." He paused. "For a reason," he added.

The salesman stopped talking and looked over the car. He handed the keys to Frank. "Look it over," he said. "Take it out for a ride if you want. I've gotta make a call." He walked across the lot, back to the sales office.

The keys felt cool in Frank's hand. He walked around the car, getting a sense of it, eyeing the headlights, mirrors, checking for signs of rust, noticing the tires' tread. It was a car that seemed to always be reaching forward. Like his old car. Stretching out into the distance. Frank made his way back around to the driver side door.

Inside the car it was quiet. For the first time in a while Frank felt safe. He wrapped his hands around the cool steering wheel. Looking out over the wheel, over the shining black hood, through the clear windshield—recently cleared of morning frost—Frank could see the highway stretching out before him, disappearing behind him like a giant concrete treadmill. He imagined the ghost of Lucinda in the passenger seat. He looked in the rearview and imagined his country's borderline. Everything meaningful that had happened to him hovered around the edges of the country he knew. He turned the key. The engine roared to life. Its sustained breath steady. Stable. Frank put it in gear and drove across the lot.

Frank laid an envelope on the salesman's desk. He was sitting behind it just as he'd been when Frank arrived. "That's more than it's worth," Frank said. "I don't like paperwork."

The salesman opened the envelope and flipped through the bills. He looked at Frank. Waiting for him to talk. Frank knew all the tricks. He had perfected them. Frank wanted to grin—admiring how the salesman had left him alone with the car, trusted him to drive the car alone, and how he was now letting the silence hover. He knew you had to be alone in the quiet to know what you wanted.

After a long quiet, the salesman smiled. "I hate paperwork, too. Where ya headed?"

"North or south. Following Buffalo."

The salesman considered this. "They're always on the move. Sometimes they disappear."

Sales Pitch

Frank and the car salesman stood in the office, feeling the post-sale ease.

"Listen," Frank said. "I used to work in sales, in a way. I got a question for you. How do you feel after you make a sale? Honestly."

"I don't know." He paused. "Guess I feel good. That's the goal, isn't it?"

"You never felt empty? Like the thing you worked toward wasn't certain. Like you weren't sure that it mattered?"

The salesman rubbed his chin. "I guess I felt that way before. But I usually don't think about it."

"But isn't it there whether you think about it or not?"

The salesman reached out a pint from his desk drawer. He smiled. "Hell, that's what this is for." He took a drink and then held it out to Frank.

"No thanks. I'm off it for a while." Frank went on. "But it's still there, isn't it? The doubt? The empty?"

"Everybody's got that. You just gotta not think about it too much. Take my cousin Charlie." He took a pull from the pint. "He's a gravedigger. Digs graves all day. Rain or shine. He can't think about what he does all the time. He'd go crazy. You see? We're all gravediggers." He laughed.

But Frank saw a glance that showed his doubt. His guilt. His lostness. Frank said: "See, in my old job, I would sell people something that would make them feel better. That would take away the gravedigger feeling. 'Cept my own grave-digger feeling never went away. It only got worse the more I helped other people."

"Maybe that's cause you weren't really helping them."

"You understand. I never knew how to really help them. Sometimes I thought I did. But it had nothing to do with what I was selling them. Not really. It was close to that but not exactly." Frank was quiet for a moment. "And the people close to me. I never could help them. I never knew how."

"You think too much."

Frank laughed. He didn't know why. Sometimes laughing was the only thing left to do. "I spent most of my life in a car like that one you sold me. Driving all over. One side of the country and back. Lot of time to think."

"Too much."

"That pint looks prettier every minute."

The salesman put the pint down on the desk. "It's there if you need it."

"Yes." Frank eyed the Ancient Age pint on the empty wood desk. The day was overcast with one thin cigarette-smoke-smear of gray cloud covering the whole sky, and pale muted light leaking through the glass storefront onto the desk. "It is."

The salesman patted Frank on the shoulder. "We'll be okay."

Frank laughed at himself. "Thanks for the car. She's a beauty." Frank looked down at his flannel shirt sleeves. "I've gotta get a suit. A man needs a suit."

"Man needs a suit," the salesman said.

North

Frank steered the black Chrysler New Yorker west along the wooded back roads until they reached the interstate. North on 75. That would take them out of harm's way. All the way into the new country. Buffalo stood in the seat with her front paws on the sill and looked out the passenger side window.

"We'll get down the road and get you some food. We're headed north. To Canada. How's that sound?"

Buffalo glanced at Frank, then went back to looking out the passenger window.

"That's true. It will be cold. But we're too old for Mexico. The north country is for old timers like us. Sitting Bull went north. Geronimo went south. Canada is for old men. But you may need to learn some French."

Buffalo ignored him and kept watching the trees go by.

"Fair point, Buffalo. There's no reason to talk to people much."

Signs, exits, fields, forests passed. The sun stayed behind clouds. Kentucky became Ohio. The light became gentler. Then headlights. Ohio became Michigan. Frank kept his speed right at the limit. At a gas station, he got gallons of water, coffee, cans of beans, reams of beef jerky, and a satchel. Every time he drank, he held out the gallon container for Buffalo to sip. He tore little pieces of jerky for her.

As they moved farther north Frank began to worry less about whether each pair of headlights they passed belonged to a state trooper.

At midnight they reached Bay City. Frank turned off the interstate. Took the sideroads toward Lake Huron. He knew, for a while, it would get more difficult before it would get easier.

The lake glowed with moonlight. With the satchel slung across his shoulder, Frank pushed the car toward the lake. The dark car inched forward, crunching gravel beneath its tires.

The Huron slowly swallowed the Chrysler. Before the car's rear window disappeared, Frank imagined Lucinda and his brother, Henry, sitting calmly inside, looking back at him. Lucinda smiled back at him from the passenger seat, her dark hair streaming over her shoulders. Henry sat in the back seat. Frank imagined that Henry's guitar, freshly stringed, was laying in the trunk, in its case, ready for the revival song chords. You're not even dead yet, Henry. What is your ghost doing here? "And you know all of life, death, and ghosts, big brother?" Henry answered in Frank's mind, his lips unmoving as he sat in the back seat of the sinking Chrysler. Henry's ghost continued calmly looking back at Frank until the water covered him and he disappeared.

Frank watched the water surface until it became a calm mirror of sky and moonlight again.

In the dark, Frank and Buffalo walked for hours until they reached the interstate. Frank eyed the narrow green mile marker 150 sign and guided Buffalo into the woods near the road. Propping his satchel like a pillow against a thick pine trunk, Frank laid down on his back in the bed of soft pine needles. He could still smell the scent of pine through the cold. He felt the burn of cold in his feet, hands, ears, and nose. Buffalo laid on his chest. He waited for sleep.

Magic City

In the dawn Frank had walked north along the edge of the interstate, carrying Buffalo. He'd hitched a ride with some fishermen headed for Canada in a black Dodge Ram. An old man was driving, and his son was sleeping in the camper top-covered truck bed. The old man sipped coffee from a steel Thermos lid cup. The old man had not said anything beyond "Where ya headed?" when Frank got in, and "Coffee?" shortly after.

Frank drank coffee from a Styrofoam cup. The sun had not yet appeared, but light was rising at their left. In a few hours they would be on a long bridge—the line between Lake Michigan and Lake Superior. And then they would be on the borderline of two countries.

Frank remembered the old magic. It was always at the edge of things. The edge between day and night. Between sunset and dusk. He could see the last light stealing in along the edges of the old canvas tent. Magic seemed effortless. But it was not. It was always planned. Honed. Carefully. One emotion built on top of another. Energy built in such a way that it would transform into belief. Into release. Catharsis. To get there, Frank used all the tools. Nostalgia. Grief. Joy. Excitement. Peace. In the right order. In the right strength. At the right time. The old songs. The new songs. The Old Testament judgment and despair. The New Testament forgive-ness and repair. The everyday stories of despair. Death. Loss. Hope. Love. Healing. Laughter. And the space between sun-set and last light was the window the magic crawled through. He led them up to it. Carefully. The more effortless it seemed the more hard work laid hidden. He had learned the path so well it became intuition. It became natural. Instinct. If it was done right, they were ready to surrender. Surrender to belief. He created that desire in them. That ability.

And in that space of change—between day and night—he showed them healing. Showed them a hint of it. Just enough that they could believe. And they could feel. After he had led them up to the edge of day and night, distracted them enough that they forgot the wonder of it, he made them see the reality of healing. Then they believed. And that was the magic. Belief. Belief in healing. That anyone could care enough to see and understand what they needed. And then, by force of will, to heal.

A shard of morning sunlight—reflected in the truck's rear-view mirror—blinded Frank. For a moment. Almost drug him back into the present. But he was too far lost in the past. Too deeply buried. He imagined it was the glare of the spotlight, illuminating him under the revival tent, casting his shadow into a distant place. He remembered how whole and warm he felt, under the bright light, moving without knowing, all instinct, his body loose and relaxed—a conduit. An instrument. He would feel the vibrations of his words ringing out in his throat, booming through the microphone he gripped in his hand. He would feel the emotion swelling through his chest, from where he did not know. He would feel his damp shirt collar against his throat, feel the cool breeze move through the revival tent, piercing between his suit coat and sweat-dampened shirt, cooling his skin. He would feel his chest rising and falling.

Then the spotlight would fan from him at the lip of the stage, under the revival tent, back to his brother, Henry, standing at the back of the stage with his Martin guitar, new silver strings shining in the light, strumming a minor chord. The first chord of a minor song. A song about grace. He imagined Henry must have felt he had a minor life.

The spotlight moved from the onstage show of healing back onto the individual. Onto the crowd. Their healing. The old farmer sitting on the metal folding chair. The young woman with dark hair, leaning forward with hands clasped, praying with her eyes squeezed tightly shut. Shifting from the staged show down into the reality of their own soul. Their healing. Their offering. Their communion. At the end everyone was left alone with their own soul. Even Frank. Even you.

And the spotlight was blinding. Burning hot in the humid southern nights. He sometimes wished it was the blinding brightness of a terrible angel wrenching him from this world. He imagined Henry smiling in the spotlight, going into a major chord, imagining a major life, carrying the magic carefully like a flame against a great wind.

Non-Magic

For the last two days Frank and Buffalo had been hiking north across Sugar Island. They'd camped under a crowd of pines the night before. The scent of pine needles was still on Frank's hands. It was late afternoon when they reached the northern edge of St. Mary's River. Rain fell down in a fine mist on the river.

Frank rowed. In slow circles, the oars rose from the water, threw water beads off into the air, moved forward and then sunk back into the water again. The canoe moved across the water.

It had stopped raining. Buffalo had come out from her dry hiding place in the satchel. She sniffed the seat of the canoe and looked up at Frank. Frank stopped rowing. The oars rested. He sighed. The river carried them slowly east. Toward the sea. Frank looked out across the river to the other shore. The new country. The sun hung low like a bright leaf about to fall off the side of the world.

Frank remembered when the magic changed. It wasn't that it went away. It was worse than that. The magic still worked. People still believed. Maybe more than ever. But Frank couldn't feel anything anymore. He had become an actor in his own life. Reading a script. Going through the right motions at the right time. Saying the right words at the right time. Evoking the effect that was needed in each moment. He didn't know what had caused this change. It had come on slowly, then all at once. Like an avalanche. Or a tornado. He wrote it off as part of getting older. Maybe he had just gotten tired, he thought. He found a way—in radio—to work that was more disconnected from people in the hope that it wouldn't show. In the hope that he wouldn't feel so bad about the distances he couldn't close. The distances that had stretched out within himself. The distances that had stretched out between himself and the world. Between himself and other people.

He felt better now. In his new life. No one expected magic of him anymore. No one expected anything. Life was simple now. He was only a walker. A former prisoner. An escape artist. A driver. A passenger. A rower. An eater. A sleeper. A follower of Buffalo. He didn't have to be anything. Buffalo looked up at him as if to say, "Why aren't you rowing?" That's how Frank interpreted her look. He smiled, picked her up and held her against his chest. She licked his nose. "Alright, girl, I'll row again." She licked his nose again. As if his decision pleased her.

Across the river Frank rowed on toward the new country. Their canoe floated on the borderline. Dusk settled down on the river like an old friend he hadn't seen in years—that he longed to rehash the old stories with. Frank listened to the oars lapping at the water.

He felt good.

Buffalo stood at the front of the canoe looking out ahead. Frank imagined he was a captain and Buffalo was his first mate. He wondered if pirates had cats. He guessed they probably did—to control mice if nothing else. Frank yelled: "Buffalo, mind the hull! Keep the sun ever at our port." Buffalo ignored him completely. Smart girl, he thought.

Imagining ancient oak chests—bursting with treasure—buried on the advancing beach, Frank rowed on.

Wilderness

In the dawn Frank saw a light ahead. His beard had grown out over the weeks he and Buffalo had been roaming northward through Ontario. He had a vision of a cabin. Like all his visions, it was enveloped by pines.

It was a country for pines. He knew he would find his cabin if he kept looking. He saw it clearly in his mind. He hoped it would appear soon. They were down to their final can of beans. Buffalo had become thin. At night they had been able to fend off the cold with fire. But one very cold, damp night could be the end for them.

In the distance laid a small open pasture surrounded by luminous pines, looking as if they were made of light. Buffalo walked ahead of Frank. He was worried about her. The last few days they had to cut their rations. Only a couple bites of beans a day. She was walking more slowly.

The scent of frying bacon reached him like news of a long shot coming in at the horse track—that you waited to be confirmed before looking at the winning ticket in your pocket. Frank and Buffalo approached the back of the large cabin— the source of light. A gravel road snaked out from the cabin and a sign glowed: "Hunters' Diner." Frank crouched and scratched Buffalo behind her ear. "I'll be right back. I'll bring you a lot of food, okay? We are close to our new home now."

***

Frank sat in a booth along the thick log cabin's wall. Booths lined three walls of the cabin. Heavy oak tables were scattered across the plain pine floor. A door in the back led to the kitchen. The rustic wood ceiling arched to a high peak. Like a chapel. Music was playing. Frank imagined it was coming from the kitchen, through a small radio above the sink. A lone bass line echoed through the big open room. Acoustic guitar chords joined the bass. Then a voice: "Hark, now hear the sailors' cry; smell the sea and feel the sky. Let your soul and spirit fly, into the mystic. And when that foghorn blows, you know I will be coming home. And when that foghorn whistle blows, I wanna hear it, I don't have to fear it."

It had been so long since Frank had heard music. In his old life music had always been with him. The waitress laid a menu and a glass of water down on the wood tabletop. Her dark French braid bobbed as she walked back into the kitchen. Frank tried not to act like he was starved: hungry for everything he saw, smelled, heard, and felt. Earlier, when he washed his hands and face in the bathroom sink, he caught his reflection in the mirror. His beard was half gray. His face was narrow. Thin. His gaze, blank. In the last year, he had become an old man.

The waitress brought out a steaming pot of coffee, a stack of pancakes, maple syrup, fried eggs—over easy, grits, and a side of bacon. Frank sat the bacon aside for Buffalo. He started with the grits. Steam rose as he stirred sugar and a pat of butter into the grits. The butter melted and disappeared.

Spooning his first bite into his mouth, he remembered the breakfasts of his childhood in Mississippi. Warmth spread through him.

He couldn't make Buffalo wait. He wrapped the bacon in a paper towel and walked outside to her. She waited at the back of the cabin. He unwrapped the bacon and set it before her, tearing it into small pieces she could chew. She took big bites and barely chewed them. Frank smiled, petted her side, then walked back in the diner.

When he returned the pats of butter on his pancakes had melted. He pierced his yolks and watched yellow bleed over white. After dashing the steaming eggs with pepper and salt he made short work of them.

Frank saved the pancakes for last. He soaked them in maple syrup and interspersed bites with pulls of hot coffee—cut with cream and sugar. After taking the last bite, his white plates cleaned, he leaned back in the booth. In his old days a cigarette would be in order. It was strange handling dead habits: they left holes that needed filled with new habits. If you filled them it was not too bad.

"How was it?" The waitress smiled, looking over his clean white plates.

"Perfect," Frank said. He noticed her dark brown eyes and the way her smile was visible in her eyes, too.

"Need anything else?"

"Always. Everything." Frank laughed.

"Just one of everything?"

"Just one. I think we could use some more supplies. Bacon. Do you have jerky?"

"Deer jerky okay?"

"Perfect. Are there any cabins for rent?"

The waitress thought it over. "Candice is in at 10. Come back then. They used to have a couple old family hunting cabins."

"Thank you."

"Clean plates, too. Good boy."

Frank laughed. "I couldn't let mom down."

"We can never do that." She stacked the clean white plates and placed the empty grits bowl on top. "That your cat I saw out there?"

"My hunting cat. Very rare breed." Frank smiled.

"Hunting cat. Never heard of that. She seems sweet."

"She's part Buffalo. All the way, really. That's her name. She's a sweetheart."

The waitress smiled. Frank looked into her brown eyes. It felt dangerous. Like looking into the sun during an eclipse. And it was. She walked away, and he missed her.

So this is what the monks feel, Frank thought.

Rest

Rest was not something Frank was good at. But Buffalo needed rest. And he needed rest, too. Frank laid on the bed in the one-room cabin. Buffalo sat on the windowsill, looking outside, feeling the warmth of the sun. The cabin had one window—that the afternoon light poured into—one wood chair, a fireplace, and a bed. Pines stood guard near the cabin. But it was not the cabin of his vision. He and Buffalo would rest here until winter was gone and spring was stable.

Every Monday morning Frank and Buffalo would wake before dawn and walk five miles to the diner to eat and get supplies for the week. Rachel—the waitress with the dark French braid—would try and set aside cans of beans and vegetables, eggs, and deer jerky. Frank would get the same breakfast—grits with melted butter and sugar, pancakes soaked in maple syrup, fried eggs—over easy, and a side of bacon for Buffalo. Rachel would tear the bacon into small pieces for Buffalo. In the dawn-dark, she would insist Buffalo come inside and eat on the booth beside Frank. Over the last months Rachel had picked up supplies for Frank in town—a backpack, jeans, hiking boots, heavy blankets, a sleeping bag, more plaid shirts. He paid her for her trouble.

Time passed.

The winter tried to change into spring. The change came in fits and starts. Rushing into warmth. And then, reconsidering, the world rushed back into cold.

Frank noticed bright dashes of yellow daffodils along his walks with Buffalo. Then white, pink, red dashes of bloom. Leaves burned bright green. And the pine needles became a dark, cool, luxuriant green. Beside their long Monday routes, they would usually walk some every day. Unless the cold was extreme. Or the rain or snow.

Buffalo was better at resting than Frank. She put her weight back on. Her gray coat became pristine, untangled. Rachel would brush her most Mondays at the diner. And she insisted on expensive canned food for Buffalo. Frank balked at the price. But it was all a show. He would rather spend money on Buffalo than himself.

Frank tried to rest, but his mind kept rushing through time and space. From the past to the future. From one ghost to another. Everyone was a ghost to him now, whether they were alive or dead. Buffalo tried to show Frank how to rest. She did not worry. From instinct, she had led Frank out of one prison. Now, she tried to show him how to escape the prison of himself. And Frank could escape sometimes. For brief moments.

Escape is always a matter of life and death. Houdini knew this. Moses and Jesus knew this. Sitting Bull knew this. At times they had all tried to dress it up. To make a show of it for the crowd. But there it was: life and death always stood in the wings like a bright, spotlighted, velvet curtain against a dark stage. Wild animals knew it. Buffalo knew it. Pines knew it. Every day they escaped death. Every season. That is why their needles clung to branches. Reached out to the sun. And their branches clung to trunks. And their roots clung to the earth—wrapped their arms around her, drank deep from her rain.

In the deep of spring, Frank and Buffalo took long walks through the woods.

Frank imagined the trees were faces in the crowds he used to try and save. Every moment he had to prove himself. Overcome doubt. Convince.

He did not have to convince Buffalo or the trees. He only had to walk and breathe. And drink from the stream that ran behind their cabin.

There were days when Frank felt free. Returning from a long walk in the woods, with the afternoon light bursting between tree limbs. Following Buffalo down the path. Going home.

Motion

By summer, Frank had begun to feel restless. His walks with Buffalo had gotten longer and pushed the limits of the time the light allowed—leaving before dawn and arriving back in full dark. In the mornings, Frank didn't want to leave his bed. In the evenings, he didn't want to go home. Instead, he wanted to keep walking—always further.

Buffalo and Frank had maxed out their one-day walking distances and had begun trying for overnight hikes. To go further. Always—north, east, or west—seeking the home of his vision: the disheveled log cabin enveloped by white pines. He began to wonder if it really existed. Could he trust his vision?

That was the problem with visions. They kept you disconnected from what was really in the world. They kept you searching for an ideal. Always searching for something that was like something else. Like something in your mind.

Frank laid down in a cool creek near the top of a mountain. It was late into the still and humid summer afternoon. Green burst from the shore like fireworks exploding over the sea—all shades from pale to rich, lush, dark tones. The stream gurgled over smooth stones. Buffalo stared at him from the shore: a patch of soft gray among the violent greens. He imagined she was judging him. Her pale green eyes pierced and searched him. Seemed to say, "What are you doing?" Prodding him to head back home. He laid on his back in the cool water and looked up. Through the dark green shadow of leaves, a smear of bright white cloud glowed.

He had not brought a sleeping bag or food. But he wanted to keep moving on. He did not care about the dark or the rules of food, nutrition and energy.

He felt reckless.

He only wanted to keep moving.

He lay still as a tree, feeling the cold water slow his heart, and thought about motion. Moving. He watched the cloud move through the leaves. The cloud passed by. And was replaced by a patch of clear and pale blue.

He laid in the cold stream for a long time.

When he stood up from the water, his hands, feet, arms, and legs were numb. Filled with cold.

He imagined the deep secret place inside the mountain where the stream came from.

Escape Artist

One summer in Kentucky, when Frank's dad was a boy, he saw the Houdini Brothers perform. His dad would often trot the story out. He would always mention how short Houdini was. Like that made him more human. Or maybe even more of a myth. And how Houdini made eye contact with everyone in the crowd. Even Frank's dad. And Frank's dad always talked about how Houdini never was as good alone as he was that summer with his brother at a little carnival in Kentucky.

King of Handcuffs, they called him. Frank's dad said that Houdini was the only great man he'd ever met. And you could tell just by seeing him in person. You could sense it. It was a kind of magic that Houdini just had. He didn't have to do anything to have it. One time someone questioned Frank's dad. Said there was no way Houdini was playing a small carnival in the year Frank's dad saw him. But Frank's dad just shook his head. "No," he'd said. "A man knows greatness. You know when you see it. It was him."

The story stuck with Frank. Long after his dad was gone. Frank wondered why it stuck with him. And why it had stuck with his dad.

Frank sat on the porch of their cabin. This had been their home the last four months. The morning light was running late. Summer raced toward fall and was beginning to lose some of her light. Just small slivers of missing light at the edges of day. Now only a sliver of dark purple severed the black horizon. Beside Frank, on the porch, leaned a heavy backpack, filled with canned beans, canned cat food, deer jerky, a canteen, peanuts, a warm sleeping bag, a map, and a compass. Buffalo sat next to Frank and looked out toward the path. She understood they were leaving again.

Frank was compelled to find his vision. He felt the cabin enveloped in pines was not far off.

They headed north.

They hiked until dusk. Frank and Buffalo slept on top of the sleeping bag. In the middle of the night, the cold came on, and Frank awoke with his ears and nose tingling with cold. He covered Buffalo with the sleeping bag.

Frank awoke to a familiar sweet-sour scent. Buffalo was licking his nose. He stretched out his arms. "You're right, Buffalo. Time to move." Buffalo ran down the path, northward, while he rolled up the sleeping bag.

For forty days, they walked in the light, slept in the dark, and drank at the streams. Their pack was light again. It was too late to turn back. Frank guessed they had enough food for another couple days. At most.

Judging by the map, Frank thought they were close to a skiing lodge in a place called Searchmont. He hoped his cabin covered in pines would be just north. An old, abandoned hunting cabin, as he imagined.

***

For two days they had no food. Buffalo began to walk slowly. Fall had overtaken summer, and the leaves were turning. He knew the cold would come soon. Only the pine needles would remain unchanged.

They couldn't keep moving for long. Their strength would go. Frank walked a pine-covered path up the foothills of yet another mountain and remembered how his dad would tell the Houdini Brothers story to him and his brother, Henry. It was one of the few times he'd seen his father excited about anything. His dad's life had been a small life. And he felt joy about the other world. The one that couldn't be seen and that he could only guess at.

But when Frank's dad talked about how he and his brother had snuck off and hitchhiked to Lexington to see the Houdini Brothers, you could hear excitement in his voice. He told them how Houdini broke his chains. Escaped from his cage. Frank's father had been in the front row. It had been the adventure of his life.

He had broken the rules. He had seen real magic.

He said when Houdini was free, he stood with his arms outstretched like Jesus on the cross. As free as a wild animal. He freed himself from ropes, chains, iron shackles, handcuffs. And at the end of his story, Frank's dad would say, "And at the end, all his magic tricks done, Houdini stood alone on the stage and said in a quiet voice that made you lean in: 'Look at this life—all mystery and magic.'" And whenever he told the story Frank's dad seemed to believe that.

When Frank got famous with his revivals, he wondered how the Houdini Brothers would see him. Would Houdini rush in with a fake beard and flip over the tables? Like he did with the spiritualists?

All of Houdini's magic was in this world. Frank's was, too. He didn't want anything to do with the other world anymore. Buffalo rubbed up against his leg, and Frank realized he had stopped walking. Buffalo walked off the trail, up a thin trace toward a grove of white pines.

Frank followed Buffalo. Up a hill following a deer trace, they arrived at a grove of pines near the peak. Frank hoped he would find the cabin of his vision here. Through the pines, Buffalo led him to a stream. There was no cabin. They drank water and laid down by the spring.

For another week they walked on through the woods. With no food. Frank became delirious. His past and present became one. His father's story and his became one. His brother and the Houdini Brothers became one. Buffalo became his brother. Buffalo became Houdini's brother. The separation between waking and sleeping worlds blurred.

There was no separation between things anymore.

Only two things remained concrete: he would keep his sense of north, and he would not abandon his brother.

When he was awake, he was aware of the change between day and night. But mostly day and night pervaded his sleep through sound: crickets and owls were night; birds were day. Buffalo—ever his guide—would wake him by scratching on nearby tree trunks or licking his face when he had slept too long into the day. And they would meander northward while they could.

Frank had finally given up hope. And planned to stay where he was lying. The steady trickling water was the soundtrack of his life draining away. He didn't have any strength to keep moving. And no desire left.

One morning Buffalo stood on his chest and incessantly pawed at his neck and shoulders, meowing urgently and desperately—unrelenting until she forced him to get up from the pine-needle ground and walk behind her, down the path. And then up yet another trace.

Near the top of the hill—on a plateau before another gradual incline up to the mountain peak—a stone chimney rose between pines. Frank picked up his pace.

Inside the pine grove laid his vision. A smaller cabin than he'd imagined. In a more severe state of disrepair. Windows broken. Sunlight streaming through a holy roof.

Frank guessed he may have slipped into the next world. And this was not real. He walked inside.

Frank brushed aside sunlight-streamed cobwebs. He knelt and opened the pantry door. Rows and rows of canned tuna, beans, mason jars with green beans, honey, jam. A steel can opener with a red handle.

He laid on the dirty cedar floor. Sunlight blasted scattered shapes onto the floor. But the room was mostly in shadow.

He sat up, leaning against the cool cabin wall, and held the can of tuna to Buffalo. She tore away large violent bites. He made her pace herself. He ate a few bites of tuna. He opened the beans and held the can out to Buffalo.

For three days, Frank ate and slept on the cedar floor. He and Buffalo would wake, eat, drink from the canteen, and drift back into sleep. Frank dreamed of the work he would do to their new home when his strength came back.

A Dream of Orion

At dawn, after three nights of sleeping on the cabin's cedar floor, Frank woke up remembering a dream. A dream so vivid he thought it was a memory.

In the dream he was young. Just starting out as a revival preacher. He and his brother, Henry, had just held a revival in an open field beside a tree-lined river in Kentucky.

In the dream it was night, and he was standing waist-deep in a river with a pretty dark-haired woman that he could not heal. They both knew she would be dead soon.

And Frank had his arm around her, pulling her body close to his. Her dress waved under the water, as if in a strong breeze. And the water was loud. It was a moonless night.

So far, the dream was a memory. Frank really had stood in this river, at night, with the dark-haired woman.

But then something new. Something that had not happened.

"I told you I'd see you again," she said.

"What do you mean?" said Frank's dream-self, ignorant of the dream world and the time gone by; he was still a nineteen-year-old kid trying to carve out a place in the world. It was still the first time his dream-self had ever met the pretty dark-haired woman, though she haunted him from the first. And she always would.

She just smiled at him. They were silent for a long time. "See the water stars?" She pointed at the stars glancing off the river's surface. "See how they wave? They're no less real than the night stars," the woman said. Frank's dream-self watched the water stars sway with the current.

He wanted to stay here with her. He didn't want to leave. He had felt the same way the first time he had met her. In the awake world.

"See Orion?" she said, pointing at the dark water. Orion's belt and shoulders gleamed on the water. "You know his story?" she said.

"He was a great hunter, right? And he hunts in the night sky forever. With his dog?"

"It should have been a cat," she said.

Frank laughed. "I always wanted a cat."

"You'll have one," she said, still staring at Orion on the water. "Orion was a great hunter. And he walked on water. And he raped a king's daughter. He was blinded by the king. Then he was healed by the goddess of dawn, who fell in love with him." The dark-haired woman pressed her finger onto the water's glass surface, scattering the image of Orion's golden pointed body. "Then, another goddess—the goddess of the moon, this time—fell in love with him. He boasted he'd kill all the animals and angered the god of healing and light. So, the God of healing and light tricked the moon goddess into killing him. And after she killed him, the goddess of the moon, who loved him, put him in the night sky to always be remembered."

"Always remembered," Frank said. Frank's dream-self watched Orion coming back together after being shattered by the woman's touch. "So he walked on water, everyone loved him, and he raped a woman?"

"And one goddess healed him, and one goddess made him immortal," she said.

"More than I can do," Frank said.

"You can do more than you know," she said.

"Sometimes I feel that I can. I know sometimes it's a put-on. Most the time. But sometimes. Sometimes it feels real. And I think I really can heal."

Again, the woman pressed her finger onto the surface of the water, and Orion's body broke into pieces. Her face was illuminated by the sky and water stars.

She looked so pretty to Frank.

"I don't know if I'm really good or bad," Frank said. "I want to be good. But I'm not very good at it."

"You can only be yourself. And good or bad doesn't matter. There's only being loved and being remembered. Or being unloved and being forgotten."

Orion had come back together, and he stood shimmering and bright on the dark water.

Part Two

Promised Land

The separation between things came back slowly. And would never come back completely. After three days of sleep, the line between waking and sleeping worlds showed itself. But it was not solid. It was a line made of steam or water. A line that could be severed. Broken.

The separation between time was the same. Unsolid and unreal. An illusion. Now the past could break through into the present.

The separation between people and objects became clear. But he could still see the illusion of a line. He guessed it may solidify over time like a pond in winter. Frank was afraid the lines would break, and, at any time, one thing would change into another: light, dark, past, present, future, himself, other, Buffalo, his brother, his mother, his father, the pines enfolding the busted cabin.

It is impossible to know what long term effect a big shock will have. Sometimes there is no effect; sometimes it only seems like there is no effect; and sometimes nothing is the same, and it is like a new self has been born. And often it is a lesser self, a lesser world.

The change to brown landscape, cold, and brief light was coming. His beloved pines were the only thing that would not change. There was a lot of work to get ready for winter. He owed it to Buffalo to make their new home like it was in his vision.

After studying the map, he realized they must be within walking distance of the ski resort at Searchmont. They could find supplies there. For the repairs. For the winter.

After a week of searching—and finding a fresh spring near their cabin—they found the resort. It was a two-day hike southeast. Frank and Buffalo made the journey back with the supplies, and it was time to get to work.

The work was good for him. It allowed him to put thinking aside. For a time. It helped his body re-capture some strength. And allowed him to make his mind a nice, clean blankness. And he could go back to the mind later. It would be waiting. He had all winter to understand.

With the dying summer sun behind him and the pines still rising above him, Frank hammered nails into the cabin roof. The holes in the roof were mended so that the sunlight, the night stars, the rain, the snow could no longer break though. At least he could repair the line between inside and outside. The broken window was boarded. With a hinge. So it could be opened when it was warm.

Frank left one of the plywood roof boards hinged on. An escape hatch if they needed it. On warm fall nights Frank would open the skylight with a birch limb and watch the stars swim by. In the morning he pulled it closed again with a rope. Buffalo loved the rope, which hung from the rigged skylight. She'd swat at it, try and climb it, and stare at it suspiciously any time it had the audacity to move in the breeze.

Frank scrubbed the floors and mended the rotting cedar floorboards. He gathered, chopped, and stacked firewood along the western cabin wall.

The night before the first freeze they had everything set. It was comfortable. Frank had gone back and found his abandoned sleeping bag. From the place where he had given up until Buffalo made him move. In the night the sleeping bag gave some ease against the firm cedar planks.

Frank sat in the cabin on the lone kitchen chair watching the small fire burning in the stone fireplace. He'd had to clear the chimney of dead doves and squirrels, rotted branches and decomposing pine needles. Buffalo laid by the fire with her front legs reaching out in front of her—flat against the cedar floorboard—watching Frank.

Frank smelled cedar and listened past the popping of burning wood, past the walls of the cabin, to the wind rustling the pines that enclosed them. That hid them from the world. Always. In every season. He remembered the house in Pineville he had imagined. And then seen. Was that vision just a prelude?

Winter

In the cabin enveloped by pines and silence, when the birds and leaves had gone, Frank began the hard work of understanding. After starting the fire in the morning Frank had the rest of the day to sit in the cabin and think. In his life he had always acted out of instinct, and now he wanted to understand. He could not rely on motion now. There was no work to distract himself. No motion. No plan. He would have to look deeply into the blurred lines that remained. He was not afraid anymore. That is, he was not afraid of being afraid.

So much of his life had not been logical. Had been based on instinct. Especially the big decisions. He knew it wasn't logical to escape from a minimum-security prison. It was absurd. Foolish. A place you'd be released from in a short time anyway. A place that was, after all, not so bad. And now, as a result, he could never return to regular life.

But he now understood why he had left. Why he had to leave. Why he had followed Buffalo down the mountain path out of that prison's weak walls. He felt it then, but now he understood. The lines between his freedom and prison had been as ghost-like as the lines now were between past/present, life/death, light/dark, self/other, inner/outer, sky/earth, his story/other stories. But he was free now. Free forever. Freer than he'd been if he'd done his time and gotten out by the book.

Because now he was free from himself. He never had to be himself again. And he was glad of that. A long time ago he had gotten tired of being himself. Tired of the sound of his own name. The sound of his own voice. And now he could never go back to his old self. They would lock him away again if he became his old self. And he was glad.

Even when he was at his peak—or what outwardly looked like his peak, when he had a voice, a face, a name people knew and admired, when he wore the finest suits of his life—tailored to his slim body, before he had started to grow old in body and spirit, when everything beautiful was offered to him at every moment—he had already begun to go through the motions. Had begun to look for a way out. On the bright day the daisy was picked he saw its petals already withered.

First it had been the routine of his revival—so carefully constructed and revised, over years, that every scene built on the last, every ritual building or evoking an emotion that built on the last, complemented, contrasted, and led up to the culminating reaction. Timing, order, last-minute adjustments and improvisations, reactions to tailor to the precise moment, place, individual, crowd.

All of it became an act. Like an actor moving through the same play night after night. Worse, a method actor who tried to forget he had immersed himself in his character. Every town melted to one. Every night melted to one. Every face in the crowd melted to one. Perhaps this was the beginning of the lines between things blurring, and his recent brush with dying had just sped the process along the rest of the way. But at the peak—when he had gotten everything he wanted—suddenly all of it became meaningless. He felt nothing. And then the feeling spread throughout his life. Like an ink pen bleeding out onto a white tablecloth. Every interaction went on cruise control. Every relationship. Every action. Every moment.

So he had changed his life. Stopped traveling. Stopped the revivals. Separated himself from his brother. Found his new country. And quickly abandoned it. Found his antenna. Started his radio work. Reaching people with his sermons and rituals over the radio waves instead of in the flesh.

And that became just as meaningless. Even faster.

He was tired.

Tired of always putting on a show. In a way, the fraud charge and prison had been a relief. But he knew if he had returned to his life, post-prison, he would always have to prove to people whether he was a fraud or God's instrument.

And he didn't want to be either. He didn't want to convince people of either. He didn't want to convince anyone of anything anymore. He'd been convincing people all his life. He'd been convincing himself.

And it had left him very tired.

Nighttime

Frank was surprised how quickly the past was swept back like a beach at low tide. Snow hung on the pine limbs around his cabin. Every few days he would walk to the spring for fresh water. Buffalo would greet him at the door when he returned—the snow was too cold and deep for her. She had tried to follow him—and to lead the way—but her legs would become stuck in the deep snow. But this didn't stop her from trying to go with him every time.

In the nighttime they'd sit on the sleeping bag in front of the fire, and Frank would tell Buffalo stories from his past. The winter wind would sail through their pines. And the fire burned so hot that Frank felt like his legs would go up in flames.

He told Buffalo about his brother—Henry—and about growing up in Mississippi. About how they'd walk to the train station and watch the pretty girls. About how they'd traveled across the country in his old Buick LeSabre. And built a following. And all the people they'd met. And about all the diners they'd eaten at. All the meals they'd had.

Mugs of coffee.
Glasses of beer.
Pints of whiskey.
Packs of Camels.

He told Buffalo about how he and Lucinda met. In another country. Buffalo had been with him at the prison when he got the news of her death.

He told Buffalo about his dad and how his dad—and his dad's brother—had seen the Houdini brothers. He explained how Houdini escaped from cages, chains, handcuffs, prisons. Frank stood in front of the fire—his shadow dangling against the cabin wall—and enacted Houdini's escape, the same way his father had. He told Buffalo that she was an escape artist, too. But more subtle. And she was no show-off.

He told Buffalo about brothers. About Cain and Abel. About how the Houdini Brothers developed their act. About how he and Henry built their revivals. About their routines and their tricks.

He told Buffalo about fathers and sons; about Abraham and Isaac; about God and Jesus; about David and Absalom. He told her he did not know why sons were always dying. Why fathers were always killing them.

He told Buffalo how friends were like brothers—told Buffalo about how David and Jonathon were like brothers. And how he and Buffalo were like brothers, too. Even though she was a cat. And a girl.

He wondered if Buffalo missed the days when he would watch the sun limp across Pine Mountain and silently smoke his Camels.

He hadn't even wanted a Camel since he left. That was his old self. His old life. The life that was gone.

He liked telling Buffalo stories about the past and the future because they made the past and the future live in the present, and they took away the line between them—which was how Frank saw reality now, anyway.

He told Buffalo about mothers. And how—even though she was a cat, and she was smaller than him, and younger— she was his mother, now. Because she had given him his new life. She was the mother of his new self.

But mostly Frank made up stories. He told Buffalo about her former life as a buffalo. How she had wandered across the country. And back. Many times. And that's how she knew all the old paths. How she always guided them. She remembered.

He told Buffalo about her life as a bird. And how she'd flown all over the world. Across the ocean.

And how he had been a pine tree. And Buffalo's nest had been in his branches. And how they had taken care of each other.

Most nights he would circle back to their life as a bird and a tree and tell a new variant. A new side story. A new adventure.

Frank told Buffalo that he thought in their next life they would be a bird and a tree again. And that they would find each other. And she could build her nest with his pine needles. And she could raise her family in the nest, safe in his branches. And he would keep the wind and the rain and the snow from her when she slept. And she would make him not feel so alone. A tree can be very alone. Especially a pine. A pine is the loneliest tree in the world. He asked Buffalo what kind of a bird she would like to be. She looked at him like he was an idiot. Which, of course, he was. And he was certain she wished he was back to his silent, Camel-smoking self.

Frank told Buffalo the reason she chased birds was because those birds had been her enemies when she was a bird. And he invented generations-long rivalries and grievances, similar to the Hatfields and McCoys. Or the Montagues and Capulets.

And circling back to their next life again, he told her that he would be a white pine. So that she would recognize him. And know his pine-needle scent. He told her that he thought she would be a dove. Because doves are gray like her. And fluffy. And chubby. And so he would recognize her, too.

Buffalo laid against his leg, ignoring him, looking at the fire. "Did you know I was a fraud, Buffalo?"

She turned and looked up at him. To him her expression seemed to say, "Are you kidding me? How could I not know? Everybody knows that."

When Buffalo looked away, back to the fire, Frank would slap the rope that hung from the ceiling hatch and set it sailing. Buffalo would notice the rope moving and crouch down, hunting it: pouncing at the rope, catching it in her paws and mouth.

Thermos

A green Thermos stood in the corner of the cabin. Stainless steel.

Narrow sunlight beams seeped through tiny cracks in the walls. And reached out across the room.

Frank laid on the cedar floor. Flat on his back. Looking up at the ceiling. His fingers felt along the rough cedar floorboards like a mouse with a broken back.

Even the smallest breach in the ceiling let in a blinding brightness. A brightness that illuminated Frank's eyelids red when he closed his eyes.

Buffalo laid on the sleeping bag against the wall, and her breathing was deep, loud, and almost-sleep.

Over the years a green Thermos like the one in the corner had been by Frank's side. Rolling across the passenger seat when he took a curve too fast. Carrying the scent of coffee and bourbon.

Frank knew the green thermos held onto the cold of the room. The cold of the season. Like a pine the thermos fought change. It slowed down time. Always preserving the moment it was filled like a time capsule.

Opening his eyes, Frank could not look away from the small holes in the ceiling bursting with light. They were stars in the day. Always holding the same constellation. Never moving. Like the thermos, unchanging. Holding onto another present.

Like a blinding angel the day stars reached down to him from the holy roof. Even when his eyes were closed. Frank shut his eyes tight. Bursts of energy like red-orange fireworks flashed, disappeared, gave birth to new flashes.

His world became a bright red curtain. Behind his eyelids. And he remembered the other times his world had been a bright red curtain. In the sun. In another country. Feeling the shadow of the steel tower that would change his life touching his cheek, knowing it would change the bright curtained world to soft velvet darkness. And feeling the silk-dark hair of the pretty girl lying beside him, against his throat and arm.

He opened his eyes. Buffalo snored. The golden beams tore across the cabin. In his mind he saw a barn from his past with light beams like this. And his brother was there.

And he wanted to be like the green thermos: never surrendering to the outside.

Like the pine, always green.

Never changing.

Spirit Rock

On the long winter nights, when Frank couldn't sleep, all his stories—real, imagined, and heard—would circle the dark space above his head like a cloud of purple martins hovering above a tractor mowing a field of tall summer grass. Like the circling birds diving down for insects stirred by the tractor's blades, so would the stories dive into Frank's mind.

One story always returned, always burrowed itself into Frank's mind.

When Frank and Henry were just getting started, just building a following across the South, carrying an old circus tent canvas and stakes in Frank's car he'd rebuilt after high school—he heard the story that would stick with him.

It was after a revival show—near the end of their first summer traveling through the South. When the dark came the first coolness of fall came with it as if the future was bleeding into the present. Their tent had already been lowered to the ground, the stakes pulled, the canvas packed away in the car's trunk for the next show.

Under the cool and moonless sky Frank leaned against his car and shared a pint of Ancient Age bourbon with an old Indian named Joe. Joe was part of their show by then. He'd been along for a few of their shows. In Texas, Tennessee. And then, Kentucky.

Just a few hours before Frank had healed Joe.

The crowd had borne witness.

Joe handed the cool glass bourbon pint to Frank. Joe rarely spoke. He nodded. The scent of whiskey reached Frank. The sweet-sour scent of decay. The cheap bourbon burned his tongue and throat. The show had been a great success. Over the last few months Joe had seen how Frank and his brother, Henry, had improved. How the crowds had grown. The offering. The effect. How the crowd had been worked into a fervor that night. How Frank had roused them to belief.

He had shown them magic.

"Spirit Rock," Joe said. He nodded. Frank handed the Ancient Age pint back. Joe nodded again. "Spirit Rock."

Frank waited for him to explain himself. Instead, Joe drank deeply from the bourbon pint and handed it back. Frank liked the feel of the cool pint in his hand. He liked the way its smell belonged to the season when the cold was just being born. When the world was still carrying the cold in her belly. Frank's tongue went numb and tingly after his next pull.

"What's Spirit Rock, Joe?"

"Old story." He paused. "You."

"You wanna tell it?"

Joe nodded. The lantern light flashed at the side of his narrow face. He motioned for Frank to give him the pint back. "Short story." He used the bourbon pint as a prop. "Three warriors. Hear of a magic place. Wolf River. Where the Great Spirit was. And if they go there—on long journey, very dangerous, very lonely—they will get what they want."

Frank wondered if this was another one of Joe's rants. He had been drinking deeply from the pint. It was hard for him and Henry to keep Joe coherent for their dusk shows—let alone, after their shows.

"Alright," Frank said. He glanced past Joe's shoulder. At the tree line beyond them that ran along the small river. He had met a girl there at the beginning of the summer. Or maybe that had been at another revival. At another place. He remembered now. It had been farther north. "So, these three warriors. They go?"

Frank eyed his watch. Henry had hitched a ride into town with a woman he knew. He had to meet him in a couple hours. "First." Joe coughed. "Tobacco. They have to give Great Spirit gift of tobacco." Joe held his hand out. Frank smiled, shook two Camels loose from his pack, handed one to Joe, put one to his mouth, and put the pack back in his left breast shirt pocket. Joe held his hand out. Frank laid his steel zippo in it. Joe's face lit up around the flame. "They travel long way," Joe said, while the zippo still lit his face. "Get to the river. See the Great Spirit. First warrior, ask to be great hunter. To provide for family. Great spirit grants it." Joe inhaled from his cigarette. "Second warrior. Has everything. No one to share with. Ask for wife. Great spirit gives him beautiful wife." Joe handed the pint back to Frank.

"So, what'd the wife look like?" Frank smiled.

"Dark hair. Very pretty. Indian. This is not the point."

Frank laughed. "Go on."

Joe nods. "That woman is not waiting by the river, Frank. Different time and place."

"What do you mean?"

Joe smiled. "Third warrior." He took a draw from his cigarette. "Thinks for a long time. What does he want? Long time thinks. Finally, he says." Joe's cigarette flashed bright red as he inhaled. "I want everything." Joe exhaled his cigarette smoke into the lantern's light. "And I want to live forever. Great spirit gets angry. This man wants too much. Great Spirit turns him into a rock. Spirit Rock." Joe laughed. "Spirit Rock." He laughed again.

Whenever the story dove down into Frank's brain, as it often did, he always heard Joe laughing, and he always saw, beyond Joe, the dark tree line against the less dark sky—a darkness against a darkness, by the river.

Not Moving

Frank's watch was still working. He wound it every morning.

All winter, when he first woke up Frank would make himself lie still—completely unmoving—for a long time on the cedar plank floor. On his back. Even when Buffalo would pounce on his chest, meow at him to move, scratch at his shoulder to get his attention—he remained still with his eyes closed. Only his lips formed a smile at her persistence.

He had to teach himself not to move.

He would feel the rough cedar against the palms of his hands. The cold making itself felt in his nose, in his hands, in his ears.

Frank felt the motion in his body. Moving from his chest to his arms. Pulsing in his head.

Go. Go. Go, it said. It was pushing him to go.

He felt his body still being pulled west, down the road, toward the next revival. Toward the next. And the next. And the next.

The feeling of motion never left him. It had remained from the early years. Lasting well into the quiet years of recording and writing radio shows.

A ball of motion rolled through him, yanking him forward. Always. Into another place. Into the next moment.

It had been there before all his movement. And now it remained. Perpetual motion holding him to its law. Not letting him off the hook.

When the motion inside him got very strong and threatened to pull him up into the cabin's ceiling, when it threatened to make him stand up and run, and leave, always leave, to the next place, the next place and the next and the next, he would press his fingers into the cedar floorboards. He would breathe the cold air and cedar scent deep into his lungs. Like it was a lit Camel.

The ball of motion that drove him—that had always driven him—never left. But after a few months of making himself still every day he stopped feeling like he would be pulled away into the sky, across the country. He felt less often like he would have to run out into the cold until his lungs burned and find a way to leave, to go, to always go, to another place, a further place, and on and on.

Frank could feel his restlessness being quelled. He had tried to quell it with so many things. For so long. Faith. Faithlessness. God. Love. Booze. Constant movement. Action. Putting more and more miles on.

Frank sighed. He felt that the motion in him—the restlessness that always pushed him into another place and another moment—could be tamed here. He opened his eyes and looked up at the rope hanging from the escape hatch in the ceiling.

Buffalo climbed on his chest. And laid down. He listened to her breathing. Almost a snore.

He felt relaxed.

The ball of motion in him settled down into a chestnut-sized ball that could only clang around within his chest and mind like a ping pong ball. Powerless. Instead of a wrecking ball that tore his lungs, heart, mind, and soul. And tore his peace.

It was as if Buffalo was helping him stay on the ground. Stay still. Crushing the restless force within him into something small and manageable.

The rope hanging from the escape hatch in the ceiling swayed for no reason that Frank could imagine.

Thaw

The snow began to leave the ground.

Frank was afraid of where spring would lead him.

He walked across the thin mucous-like layer of melting snow that covered the path. Behind him mud boot prints appeared. Frank carried two tin pails.

When he reached the turn for the spring—instead of going left up the deer trace—he continued down the path. He left his pails at the spring trace.

The snowy path was full of tracks. He imagined they belonged to deer, raccoon, possum, birds, squirrels, and bear. It had been three days since the last snow.

He walked on for a long time. Until he reached another deer trace. He hiked up this trace until he stood before a stream. It was a familiar place. He looked at the pine he'd laid under for days. When he had been lost deep in fever. Past hope. At peace with dying. He recognized the sound of the stream. It was louder now, more forceful from the melting snow.

He laid down under the pine. And clasped his hands together at his chest. Closed his eyes. Listened. The familiar sound of running water blended with the sound of melting snow dripping to the ground from high branches. There was no pattern to the dripping snow. It was the time for snow to change into water. But every patch of snow that hung onto every branch changed at its own pace. The dripping sound was all at once and gradual and always returning.

The sun could not reach him here. He thought there must be another spring close by.

Buffalo ran into his mind. He remembered her making him leave this place. And leading him to their home. He smiled. He opened his eyes and looked up through the snow-covered pine limbs. The wet snow muted the scent of pine needles and hid his pine needle bed. He looked forward to the days of spring when Buffalo could walk with him again. He stood up and felt the wetness on his back, seat, and legs.

The dripping sound of melting snow got louder along the path back home.

Opening the cabin's front door—a pail in each hand— Buffalo crowded his feet and stood on her back legs to look into the water.

Later that night Frank listened again to the dripping sound of melting snow. There was still no pattern. But the dripping sound had quickened like a hard summer rain.

It was the sound of change.

Spring

The snow had been gone for several weeks. Beyond their white pines, which encircled the cabin, poplars and maples—interspersed with spruce and jack pine—wore their bright new green. The false spring had passed.

In the cabin Frank sat on the lone wood chair and rubbed his rough beard. He looked down at Buffalo. "Why have you been so quiet, girl?" Buffalo laid at his feet looking up. "Alright, it's time. We'll re-stock." She looked at the white ashen logs left over from their last fire a week ago.

Frank sat in the barber chair. Outside, Searchmont Street was empty. The street was filled with apprehension. As if winter would return. It was a ski town, and the ski crowds wouldn't come back for a while. He watched Buffalo through the barbershop window. She was laying on a wood bench to get away from the cold coming up from the concrete. She had glanced at him when he sat down at the barber chair. Now she looked out at the street. Like a sentry. On the hike in she had led the way. Slowly. Very slowly. He hoped it was the winter stillness in her and that her strength would come back with their hikes now that the weather would allow it.

Searchmont had the ski resort at the top of the mountain and one main road beneath. On the road was a barbershop, a pub, a hotel, and a post office. Frank had seen his man at the hotel first. Had ordered supplies that he'd come back for later. Supplies that would get them through spring and half of summer.

Again Frank looked out the window at Buffalo and the road. It was like a Canadian Tombstone. The old west. A set in a Clint Eastwood movie. The bare minimum. It was hardly a town at all. The barber's scissors clipped at Frank's beard. Strands of gray-black hair fell to the floor around him. Covering the floor like a light snow. "You a real mountain man, eh?" said the barber.

"Oh, I'm only half real." Frank looked down at the black chair cloth that draped his shoulders, chest, arms, torso, and legs. It was covered with parts of himself that had been cut away.

"Half is not bad. You stayin' round Ontario long?" The scissors snapped together and another strand of Frank's beard drifted to the floor.

"As long as possible," Frank said. He realized suddenly —even though he was making small talk—that he meant it. He would stay here as long as possible. And any other time in his life, any other place, he couldn't wait to leave. To leave wherever he was at the moment. To escape. To move. But now he realized that he never wanted to leave. He would stay. As long as he could. He felt in that moment—sitting there beneath the heavy black cloth looking out at the Ontario spring afternoon, feeling sweat bead between his upper arm and ribcage—a strong sense of impermanence. Like even the moment he was in right then—sitting there in the barber's chair, his beard falling apart beneath him—was already over.

But he wanted it to last.

He noticed Buffalo watching a new green leaf blowing across the road on the hard spring wind.

Her ear twitched as if it were a bird.

Frank smiled.

The barber had moved to the straight razor. Scraped it along Frank's face. Rinsed it in hot water. Frank stared at the new leaf blowing down the road. It was almost out of sight.

The barber held up a mirror in front of Frank's face. Frank saw himself. He recognized a version of himself. A new version. His face was thinner. His eyes had changed. Their expression was new. He could not explain the difference. He could not recognize that part of himself.

Frank nodded. The barber pulled the black cloth off him. Frank stood, fished a handful of dollars from his pocket and walked out.

Frank had carried Buffalo up the steep hill to the hotel lobby. She seemed very tired now. He carried her inside the lobby and walked to the concierge. It was empty. Frank only wanted to see this place in the offseason, like it was now.

The concierge appeared, wearing a black tie and coat. "Yes, we have most of your supplies now. If you can come back next week, we will have everything."

"Alright."

"This your friend?" The concierge pointed at Buffalo.

"Oh yes. She is a brave navigator. Like Shackleton."

"I see."

"So what's the best food you can get for her?"

"Hmm, yes. I can see. I will find out. You want to purchase?"

"Yes. Find the best. Price doesn't matter. Do you know a vet?"

"We have a regular. Comes in June. He can help?"

"Okay. I'll be back next week."

Buffalo looked out at the sweeping resort lobby. Frank fished dollars from his pocket.

Frank carried Buffalo all the way home. She did not seem to want to walk. "I saw the way you looked at that resort lobby, Buffalo. Are you saying you want to go skiing? You know they do that in the snow, right?" Buffalo rubbed her face against Frank's smooth new face.

By the time they got back home, Buffalo had fallen asleep. Frank laid her in the sleeping bag. She stretched and laid down.

Windows

In the morning, after boiling water and coffee grounds in an iron pot over the fire, Frank would sit in the wood chair and look out the open window. Buffalo would sit on his leg or the sill and look out, too. They would sit and watch the light and morning sounds being born in the world outside the window. The world of sounds changed from a lone owl in the distance to a chorus of chirping birds. The sound of bird calls rode in on the new light until it reached Buffalo and Frank at their window.

Whenever a bird got too close Buffalo would cock her head and become stiff like she was ready to pounce.

They got to know some of them. Two blue jays would always come to the same white pine branch outside their window in the mid-morning when the light was full. A couple of doves would walk along the pine needle ground between the cabin and pines. Just beyond the pines a family of five red-winged blackbirds perched high in a maple. Many small sparrows and occasional bright yellow birds would land on their pines.

Through his Buick LeSabre windows, Frank and his brother, Henry, had watched landscapes pass by for nearly a decade. Now he and Buffalo watched the light and animals move by. Instead of engines, music, and the purring of air-conditioned motel rooms, it was morning bird calls, Buffalo's deep breathing, and the night sounds of wind, wolves, and far-off owls.

Frank and Buffalo watched out the window until his coffee was gone, and Buffalo was asleep in his lap. When Frank was so tired he couldn't sit any more, he would lay down in the sleeping bag. Breathing the old cedar floorboard scent he looked out their escape hatch in the ceiling. And watched the sky. Buffalo laid on his chest or at his side. Through the open escape hatch the sky would change from bright blue, or smudge gray cloud, or bright white cloud. And Frank would watch it change. Some days it would remain blue most of the late morning. He watched the sky until his eyes became too tired.

When Frank awoke from his nap he'd walk down the path to the spring for fresh water. These days Buffalo would rarely go with him. She would rest until he returned.

After eating their dinner of beans, jerky, or canned tuna—or whatever Frank could get Buffalo interested in eating—Frank and Buffalo would return to the cabin's open window and watch the light disconnecting itself from the trees, animals, ground, and clouds. The gold light appeared upon and then faded from every object like the confidence of late youth. Frank and Buffalo watched every tree, bird, and cloud become luminous with the soft dusk light and briefly changed like a prizefighter in the camera flash after a winning bout.

And then the dark fell upon the world outside and inside their window. Only blinking stars or a moon that was growing or fading in a clear sky remained. Or the suggestion of star and moonlight behind the veil of dimly glowing cloud-smear sky.

As the dark went on Frank felt the air through the window cooling. He rubbed Buffalo behind her ears while she laid on his lap. Frank and Buffalo listened to the night sounds come through the window for a long time. Frank's mind was superglued to the moment. All that passed through his mind was an awareness of himself and Buffalo on this side of the window and the rest of the objects and animals in the world outside it—only the ones they could see.

When Buffalo's purr had changed into a deep snore and Frank could hardly hold open his eyes, he'd move from the chair to the sleeping bag. Buffalo would stretch out her front legs in front of her and then follow Frank across the cedar floor.

Staring up through the square patch of night sky revealed by their window in the roof—their escape hatch—Frank watched the heavens pass: the dark was penetrated by patches of stars and clouds holding the mirror light of stars and moon.

Frank felt Buffalo's body rising and falling with her breathing against the crook of his left arm and ribs.

Almost Summer

When spring's bloom reached its zenith, and the maple and poplar leaves had become a mature dark green, Frank started having a recurring dream: he would wake up in his cabin and see Buffalo rising up from the sleeping bag on the rough cedar floor and floating up through the escape hatch window in the roof—slowly rising higher and higher—and disappearing beyond, into the night sky. In the dream Frank laid in his sleeping bag, smelling cedar and looking up, staring after Buffalo for a long time. In some dream variations he would yell her name and try to get her to stay. To come back.

All through the spring's violent blooming, Frank had made solitary hikes into Searchmont to get medicine from his man at the hotel—whose vet friend had shipped it.

But the medicine didn't help any more.

When Buffalo shook from cold in the warm late spring, Frank would sit in the kitchen chair and hold her close to his chest to warm her. After she was warmer, she could relax and look out their open window at the mourning doves, robins, and red-winged blackbirds.

The trips to the spring for water became hurried. Frank did not want to leave Buffalo alone for long.

Some days in the late afternoon, when she was glowing and happy in the bright sunlight that fell through the open window, Buffalo would even glance at the rope hanging from the escape hatch as if considering an attack on her old foe.

Weeks passed.

For three days Buffalo slept almost continually. And when she was awake her body could not stop shaking. Frank stayed with her, sitting beside her on the cedar floor with his back against the cabin wall—while she lay sleeping, wrapped warmly in the sleeping bag—and tried to give her some comfort. In a quiet voice he told her the old stories about their old life. He stroked behind her ears.

Deep in the night of the third day Frank's recurring dream returned. In his dream he watched Buffalo rise up from the cedar floorboards and float slowly upward, pass through the escape hatch window, over their cabin, over their pines, and toward the heavens. He knew he would never see her again. In the dream, he wanted to follow her up, through the sky, on to the next world, letting her lead him the way she'd led him out of Pine Mountain to freedom. But he could not move.

When he woke from the dream Buffalo was gone. Her little body lay beside him. Still. At peace.

She no longer shook.

He carried her to the window and held her, watching the sunlight bloom one last time through their window.

When the sunbeams feathered out across the clouds and trees, Frank carried Buffalo down the path to the pine where he had almost died. Before they had found their home. The place Buffalo had roused him from.

He used a cool, sharp-edged rock to dig a place for her under the pine.

Buffalo rested there.

Part Three

South

The Greyhound bus rattled into the outskirts of Sault Ste. Marie, Ontario, a border town split in half by a river between two countries. Pulling his head away from the cool glass bus window, Frank drank whiskey from a steel flask. He pocketed the flask in his coat pocket. Looking out the window, Frank saw that the landscape had changed into neighborhoods and shops.

Outside the bus window Frank watched the neighborhoods and isolated shops connected with grass lawns transform themselves into closely-knit office buildings, restaurants, and bars—connected with concrete sidewalks. Downtown.

Hissing like a hurt animal the bus screeched to a full stop. Carrying his satchel over his shoulder Frank stepped down off the bus and breathed in the old smell of exhaust.

Standing on the sidewalk in Sault Ste. Marie, listening to the bus engine roar to life—loud and angry, then gradually quiet as it moved away—Frank wondered where he would go.

There was no Buffalo to lead the way.

With the lack of any better idea Frank thought he needed a suit. And he thought he'd stay on the edge of things: life, countries, people, and anything else that came up. He felt safe on the edge. It was what he knew.

In his new used gray suit, which hung loosely on him, Frank leaned his forearms against the hotel bar and slouched over his scotch. The dark mahogany bar stretched across the long wall in the dimly lit bar. The bartender had disappeared behind the bar into the kitchen, and a couple people sat drinking in booths like distant shadows in the underworld.

The light that pressed against the heavy drawn window blinds had softened. And the light outside must have been close to matching the dim light inside. Frank was damn glad that the bar was mahogany—and not cedar. He could not think of cedar. He could not think of the smell of cedar. Or the smell of pine. He was glad that the blinds were drawn. He could not face open windows. He only wanted to slip along between things. And be unnoticed. And not notice anything.

When the bar closed Frank laid on his hotel bed. A Clint Eastwood movie was on TV. Eastwood had survived a hanging. Frank was only half paying attention. To distract himself until sleep came. The blinds were drawn in his room, but shades of red neon light slivered through the sides, giving the room a red tint. And the sound of cars going by, and the air conditioner humming was alien to him and reminded him he was back in an unrecognizable world that he had no desire for. He tried to block out the sound. The sound of cars splashing by on the road outside brought reality crashing into him. Where he had been. Where he was now. Where he was going. He did not want to think of those things.

His head swam with whiskey.

The light from the TV flashed out into the darkness of the room licking the shadows like flames.

He closed his eyes and waited to escape into sleep.

Sault Ste. Marie, Ontario

Sprawled on top of the covers of the hotel bed—still wearing his gray suit—Frank slept past noon. The red neon tint of the room faded, and the terrible blinding whiteness of daylight screamed through the edges of the drawn blinds.

The sound of the terrible loneliness of moving cars outside battered at his mind. The poor machines cried out, pushed endlessly from destination to destination. When would they rest?

Frank clasped his hands over his chest—feeling the rough cheap fabric of his wrinkled tie, shirt, and sports coat—and watched the ceiling. The off-white, dimpled patterns stood out like scars or topographical maps. Imagining they were energy fields of living things, Frank made up lives for each of them. He imagined the fear and love they felt for each other. How they lamented the space and time between them.

By late afternoon—judging by the changing light which still tore through the edges of the cheap blinds—Frank's stomach demanded food. He ordered a sandwich and a bottle of port wine from room service. What kind of sandwich, they had asked. He did not care, he had said.

After eating half of the turkey sandwich, Frank took off his clothes and got under the covers. He wished the annoying daylight—which would not stop tearing through the window blinds' edges—would go away. The daylight clawed incessantly at the edges of the room like a terrible, uninvited angel on the door of a nonbeliever. The room was only half-dark.

Laying in the hotel bed Frank drank at the bottle of port wine and waited for dark to come. Gradually the red neon tint returned to his hotel room.

When the bottle was empty Frank waited for sleep. If it did not come soon, he would order another bottle. The terrible loneliness of the moving cars outside dripped on and on and on and on like a faucet in a run-down apartment that a poor plumber had given up on.

In the same way Frank spent two more days in the hotel room. The scar constellations on the ceiling had become familiar to him. Each had a name and a story. The ceiling constellation just above his head was a waitress named Loretta with hazel eyes, whose father had been a farmer. She'd left the farm she grew up on for the closest big city. Her father, Charlie, was a few constellations over.

On the fourth day Frank woke up before dawn and took a shower. "I have to keep moving," he told himself, aloud, standing under the hot water.

Rowing

Through the dawn, Frank had walked along the edge of St. Mary's River. Near noon, he walked along the outskirts of town, along a dirty stretch of shore filled with abandoned tires and Styrofoam cups. The sky was a foul gray—threatening rain, and the wind picked up, making the river choppy.

Frank found a dirty overturned canoe with one oar laying in the mud amidst debris and trash on the riverside. He righted the canoe.

A black cat bounded out. He called after the cat, and it paused, looked at him with suspicion, and then ran away.

Setting the canoe on the water, it did not sink. In his gray suit, Frank climbed in and started rowing across St. Mary's River. With his one oar, he alternated from the port to the starboard side.

His satchel—empty of everything except money—laid on the floor of the canoe.

By the time Frank reached the middle of St. Mary's River, a violent rain poured from the sky. The wind blew cold pellets of rain that stung his face.

Frank reached his steel flask out from his inside suit coat pocket and took a long pull.

Then he went on rowing.

***

In the rain, Frank wept and rowed across the dirty river. He was nearly back in America.

Sault Ste. Marie, Michigan

After sending his suit out to be cleaned, Frank laid on a hotel bed in a dim room, with the air conditioner humming and thumbed through the yellow pages. He dialed one used car lot after another; he was looking for a pale imitation of his former car—just as he had found a lackluster imitation of his former suit, just as he had become a hollow version of his former self. What else was there to do? Isn't this what everyone does every day of their lives?

After five phone calls Frank found his mark: a black Buick LeSabre. The salesman said it was a '59 model, but Frank hardly believed him. But he pretended to. And he even convinced himself that he believed, somehow. The salesman had refused to talk money, but Frank made him. Eyeing his satchel lying on the floor beside the bed, Frank knew that if he got the car for a reasonable price, he would have enough to get by for another couple months. That was enough.

The local paper—*Central Michigan Life*—laid on the nightstand beside the bed. Frank picked up the paper. He eyed the date along the top edge: September 21, 1979. That can't be right. How long was he in the last hotel? How long in the cabin after he and Buffalo went to Searchmont? He felt like he'd lost several months. Even the year felt wrong. 1979. His car—the one that carried him and his brother through their peak—was twenty years old now. Fearfully, Frank eyed the first few newsprint pages: an ad for a church—"Invitation for Worship" that promised to offer "Equipment for Living".

Equipment for living? How practical, Frank thought. How easier it must be now. They had needed, no, demanded, some sort of miracle from Frank—a handful of heaven snatched down into this world for them. Healing. Magic. Understanding. Love. Now, equipment for living would do. And they didn't need to move from town to town, building trust from strangers—no, they simply placed an ad in the paper— for a heavy price, Frank was sure—and waited to parcel out their practical equipment for living. They were selling houses with windows, no walls, no ceilings, no structure, no foundation, and no floors. Why should someone want equipment for living when they had no reason to live? When they had no magic? No faith? No confidence? No belief? They would simply set their equipment for living on cruise control and set out mindlessly on the sea, watching the scenery and clock hands spin past.

Flipping through the next few newsprint pages, other headlines were the past repeating, endlessly—Russian troops in Cuba, Kennedy's life threatened (yet a different Kennedy this time) in his bid for president, lack of confidence in the US Dollar. Lack of confidence. How was lack of confidence different from lack of faith? To Frank, there was no difference. That's what time did. Time made you lose confidence. Lose faith. In yourself. In the world. In God. In people. In everything. It made things break apart. The numbers changed, the methods changed, but the heart of things stayed the same.

He had no place in this world anymore. Disgusted, he threw the newspaper on the floor.

He drank whiskey from his steel flask.

Life in Reverse

From the driver seat, looking out over the hood of the '59 Buick LeSabre, Frank could see the dents and how the black paint had nearly faded to gray. But he ignored those details. He imagined the car was brand new, and he imagined that he and the LeSabre were setting out to make their way in the world, to show people the magic in the world. He could even keep the illusion up for stretches of time. Brief bites of time. He imagined a Camel cigarette in his left hand and smoke streaming out the driver side window.

In Kentucky, he pulled off Interstate 75. His brother, Henry, used to have a church here. It was late afternoon. His brother had put down a permanent tent, in one place, when their revivals had ended. When Frank's distant radio revival life had begun.

Frank wheeled the LeSabre around town. Perfectly manicured, golf-course-like horse farms surrounded by immaculately white horse fences blurred past him. None of their color had faded. Dark green lawns. Deeply bright white fences. A cemetery on a hill. He felt close. He would know his brother's church by sight, even though he'd never been there. His LeSabre rolled down the hill that led to the valley. There it was. Ahead, on his right. Frank's Buick slid closer. The church had a steep roof that nearly reached all the way down to the earth. Like a revival tent. And there was that word, already glowing under the setting sun: REVIVAL. The letters gleamed. It was that brief and transitory moment when objects were made gold by the escaping sun. Like alchemy. Magic time, they had called it. Each of their old revival shows was built around that moment.

Frank pulled into the parking lot of a shopping center across from the church. He loved the feeling of this place. This valley. The lot descended from a steep embankment. Frank parked his Buick in a gym parking lot. Behind the gym was a plasma donation center. Frank eyed the lost souls, too warmly dressed for the warm September day, hovering around the plasma center door. To his right, Frank could see the cemetery gate at the top of the hill. He could still see part of his brother's church directly across the street. Only the tall peak showed above the steep embankment. Frank looked up from the low side of the valley. The embankment made him feel safe. It was always this way. His back to the wall in a diner. As if every moment in his life was a subconscious preparation for battle.

He glanced up again at the peak of the Revival church. His brother's church. Its black shingled roof glowed with the desperate bright rays of the sun just before its escape.

Frank thought of the hidden sign, across the road. RE-VIVAL. Revive. To revive. To bring back to life. To bring back to life. Back to life. Back. Life. That's what he and his brother, Henry, had done for people. Strangers. Again and again. And now they give people equipment for living. Without ever bothering to bring them back to life to begin with. How can you use equipment for living when you are not alive? And who would bring him back to life? But it was something Frank knew he didn't want.

He flipped on the radio. Behind him, the plasma donation building was now draped in velvety shadow. The embankment before him was dim. But the light still showed at the peak of his brother's church. He flipped the radio dial. A piano chord sounded. Then changed into another. And a guitar line struck against the piano chords. A telecaster. A telecaster that wanted to be a steel guitar. And an organ drifted in over it all like a fog on a river. Frank listened closely to the verse and chorus—the piano, telecaster, and organ swirling around each other—until the chorus repeated one final time: "How long have I been sleeping? How long have I been drifting alone through the night? How long have I been running for that morning flight, through the whispered promises and the changing light, in the bed where we both lie, late for the sky?" The song fell back into piano chords and a telecaster crying out like a human voice, all bathed in fog.

When the song ended, Frank turned the radio off. He got a strange feeling in this place. The way he used to feel. He thought of the lady wearing a London Fog raincoat and gloves, in his rearview, walking away from the plasma building. And how, with the small change she'd earned, she would likely seek something to soothe her. He thought of the people in the gym. The scent of iron and sweat. He imagined friendships and rituals of the people inside. Losses. Always permanent. He imagined the man who owned the gym. How he was reviving people, too. Frank knew how he felt. He knew you had to give everything to convince people to be revived. Even though it's what they wanted. They had to be convinced it was possible. That was the hardest part.

Frank leaned back in the car seat and closed his eyes. The gold light blanket that covered the roof of his brother's church had been pulled back. Now it was all a cool shadow. He felt very tired. Had he seen a liquor store across from the cemetery on the hill? On the way in? Drifting into sleep, Frank dreamed of finding a beer.

And then his dream turned dark.

You've Killed Your Brother

Frank's body lay asleep, unmoving, in the faded Buick while he went from place to place trying to find a beer. In vain. He felt strange. The world and himself were not quite right. Not reliable. Had he already been drinking and couldn't remember? He walked into a room. His mother was there. She was crying.

"Frank," she said. She put her arm on his shoulder. "You've killed your brother."

"What do you mean? Is he dead? Where is he?"

"You hurt him. It's his head. He doesn't have much time." She put her hands on Frank's shoulders and guided him into another room. His brother stood in front of him.

"Henry, what's wrong?" Frank said.

"I don't know," Henry said.

Frank's brother's head was shaved, as if he'd had surgery. His skull was flat at the top, dented, like he had received a terrible blow. Frank felt he had done this. He felt responsible. But he could not remember anything beyond looking for a beer.

"Did I hurt you? Mom said I did. I can't remember. Did I do this?" Frank felt they must have fought. He remembered the anger of his childhood. The fights. He thought of the things inside him that he hated.

"I can't remember, Frank." Henry rubbed his bald head. "I can't remember anything. I'm not mad."

"I know. I'm so sorry. I feel I did hurt you. And they said so."

"It's okay. I can't remember," Henry said. His face looked bloated, and his bald, warped head looked like part of him but also not like him at all. Frank thought of the times that his brother had been in trouble. The times Frank showed him how to get into trouble. The times he could have helped him. The times he didn't know how. Or even that there was trouble. So he did nothing. The times that he left him behind. To fend for himself. Forging his own way. Jesus.

Frank hugged Henry. And he started to cry. "I'm sorry. I'm sorry. I can't remember. But they said it. They said I hurt you. And I feel like I did this. I'm so sorry. For everything."

"It's okay. I can't remember anything."

Frank woke up in the driver seat of the LeSabre, in the darkness of the valley, with the image of his dying brother. The image of his damaged, bald head. It was awful.

He turned the key in the ignition and prayed that the liquor store on the hill was open. He had to escape. From this feeling. This awful image. Full of truth and horror. His dying brother. His mother's words. You've killed your brother.

Farther Down

Waking up, Frank looked around him: empty Coors cans and a pint of blackberry brandy laid on the floor beneath the passenger seat. Morning sunlight filled the Buick LeSabre. His car faced an embankment and blinding light attacked his rearview. Squinting into the white light in the mirror, Frank saw people hovering around the plasma donation building like buzzards circling a possum corpse in the road. One man pushed a cart and wore a winter coat and old athletic shoes; another man stood stroking his unkempt beard, pausing to lean and cough, his back against the sun. At Frank's right, the gym was still and several cars were parked—their owners already inside improving themselves.

The LeSabre and Frank drifted along roads until they found the interstate. When Frank saw the end of his LeSabre stretching out towards I-75, he felt more at ease. Last night's alcohol still swam in his blood, making his head light and unclear, a harbinger of the pain to come. He knew the pain would enter his temples like thick needles piercing his skull. And that the ache would spread through his blood to the rest of his body—in the same way pleasure and release had spread the night before.

When he eyed the Denny's sign at the next exit, there was a rising uneasy feeling in his stomach. No, there would be no food for now.

The Buick carried Frank another thirty miles. After pulling off at a liquor store to pick up three liters of red wine, they were back on the road.

Frank's hand shook, and he raised the bottle to his lips. The red wine felt cool on his dry tongue and throat. He kept the bottle in his lap, holding it still with his left hand while he steered with his right.

Turning off 75, Frank followed 461. Farther south. The wine dulled the pain from the stabbing needle in his temple, and its poison spread down through his body. Along the road open fields baked in the sun. He wondered if he could remember the way.

He saw 80W and took it. A few minutes later, 90W. He turned again. He drank from the wine bottle. The LeSabre and Frank rolled down the highway, rushing past tall pines and oaks, past open fields. The clouds threw their shadow over the fields and woods. It was one of those hot days in late fall. That reminded you that you weren't out of the woods yet.

Frank rolled down his window and rested his arm on the sill. Some heat, leftover from the bright morning, warmed his forearm. Wind tore through the interior. Frank felt good. He remembered the first time he made this drive. In his first car, before the LeSabre. Henry had been in the passenger seat, the old Ringling Brothers canvas in the trunk, along with Henry's old guitar. He had been thinking over every detail for their revival. Worrying over exactly what to say. When. And how to move through the show. How to win over the crowd. He remembered how confident he had felt that they would win them. Even though he was so new at that life.

Looking over at the empty passenger seat, remembering, Frank smiled.

The faded gray LeSabre seemed to drive itself to the site of their revival almost forty years ago. The LeSabre carried Frank and his wine like a train on a track.

It was midday when Frank reached the place that had become sacred to him.

Standing up, Frank patted the roof of the Buick and walked out toward the center of the field. He had expected this place would be gone. Maybe a neighborhood in its place. But it was mostly the same. Unlike Frank and the LeSabre, this place had not changed.

Wiping his mouth on the sleeve of his gray suit coat, after taking a deep drink of wine, Frank surveyed the space. He could see the space where he and his brother's canvas tent had stood. Farther down, over the hill, Frank eyed the tree line that covered the river.

Carrying his cool, half-full bottle of wine, he walked on towards the tree line. Pines interspersed with oak, maple, birch, sycamore. The swaying yellow grass of the field reached his knees.

Walking down the rocky path, Frank stopped when he reached the river's edge. He remembered a woman. An older woman that had led him here. And he had sung to her, while she stood in the moonlit river, dying.

The water of the river was as cold as iced tea and turned Frank's feet and legs numb. When he reached the middle, he was submerged to his chest. He stood in the river and took a deep drink from the cool wine bottle. A sunbeam broke between clouds and felt warm on his face. Against the current, he fought to stand still. The sound of the river was loud in his ears. In the current, his suit coat swept behind him like it was caught in a great wind.

He wanted to stay here for a long time. At least for a while after the bottle was empty.

Fallen Barn

Waking at first light, Frank stood up and looked over the morning field. He brushed the grass from his gray suit slacks and coat. He eyed the tree line wrapping around the river. He remembered they had kept the tree line and river to the right of their stage, so that the setting sun would take its final limp at their backs. Now the morning sunlight streamed along the tree line, making no shadow.

After raising his arms over his head and taking a deep breath, Frank turned from the riverside and walked back to his car. In the gentle early morning light, the LeSabre looked like it belonged—its dark gray brushed against the tall yellow grass like Van Gogh's crows in a wheatfield.

Frank and his LeSabre headed south. The morning sun shot through the driver side window and reflected off the remaining wine bottle laying in the passenger seat. He made it twenty miles before the bottle was opened.

The third drink brought a calm into his pulsing head, aching stomach, and trembling limbs.

Like instinct Frank followed the same roads south that he had in his youth. With his brother. The LeSabre cut through fields of tobacco, corn, and blank space.

***

When he turned a corner, the wreckage caught his eye. It was almost noon. The sky was pale and clear.

The wreck of an old barn stood out like a mountain of dead lumber.

When Frank and Henry had first come this way it had been new. The LeSabre slowed, and Frank eyed the stretching mess of faded black planks fallen in on themselves.

Frank watched the wreckage in his rear view. He imagined the mess would be left to rot the way it had been left to fall apart. He imagined ivy and weeds growing all through the wreck of wasted wood that had been a barn, with all manner of animals living inside its labyrinthian sanctuary, and, over time, the planks disintegrating into a fine dark dust.

South, West

The LeSabre and Frank stuck to the back roads and headed south.

He turned off at the old revival sites along the way. Some remained as they had been. Some were now shopping centers. Some were neighborhoods. Some were churches with solid walls, concrete foundations, and shingled roofs where the canvas tent, stakes, and grass floor had been. People were being brought back to life by other methods, Frank supposed. If they were being brought back to life at all.

Always in the sun-blasted passenger seat lay a green thermos and at least one bottle of wine—or something stronger.

When it couldn't be helped, Frank and the LeSabre would pull off the road, pausing their endless motion, to refuel: 87 Unleaded for the LeSabre; hot coffee, eggs, and oatmeal for Frank.

Gasoline fumes, like tiny transparent bubbles, would rise up from the gas tank into the warm air.

Clouds of steam would rise from Frank's white coffee mug like a hovering fog escaping from the smooth black coffee pool. Eggs over easy, spilling thick yellow yolk. And the waitresses moving between table and kitchen. It was as if they had all combined into one; there was no longer any separation between them, or between the first trips south and this final one. Old, young, pretty, rough, they were all so kind. They always had been. Angels of the road. He would miss them.

When he'd gone south a while, and was close to the coast, Frank steered the LeSabre west. The last few nights had turned cold. Fall was close. But the warmth of the west dampened any clarity about the season.

The bright road, blasted with sunlight, looked like high summer, but Frank knew it was much later. Trying to save money, Frank would only stay in a cheap motel every other night, if that. Louisiana had given way to Texas.

Moving across Texas, Frank wished the landscape would change into desert sooner. It had always been this way. He and Henry had cursed the distances in Texas, too.

When he finally reached the easy, smooth, round powder edges and flat reaches of west Texas, he regretted rushing it.

He wanted to keep going west, back into New Mexico, Arizona, and Nogales again. But another place from his past was calling him.

The air-conditioned El Paso motel room beat back the lingering late day heat. Frank sat on the edge of the bed, thumbing through the phone book. His LeSabre rested in the lot outside. His gray suit had been dropped off at the cleaners. He was clean from the shower, wearing a pair of crisp blue jeans and a white T-shirt he'd found at a secondhand store at the edge of town.

***

The arrangements had been made. In the morning Frank's old friend would usher him across the border into Ciudad Juárez. Frank laid in the motel bed and watched the drawn blinds—glowing with sunlight—become dim.

The light was almost gone.

Ciudad Juárez

The LeSabre and Frank slipped across the borderline between the US and Mexico.

The first time Frank had crossed this line, he returned to find his mother gone and had to start the dirty business of building a life. The second time he had crossed this line, he returned with a pretty, dark-haired girl on his arm and a future that stretched out into the airwaves reaching further than he could imagine—making his former life unrecognizable.

But this time Frank was not afraid of losing or gaining anything that would only slip away. He would not change. He knew himself and was only coming to remember. And to feel the palpable electric charge of what had been. A reminder of what life had been when he possessed both confidence and faith: in himself, in the future, in people, in the world.

It was as if everyone had a finite amount of faith and energy. And when it was gone, it would not come back. And Frank had to have so much—not just for himself, but for everyone else: he had to make them believe. And it had all run dry in him like a spring gone empty.

The morning was hot. And clouds threatened rain, although in his memory it was always sunny and clear here.

He found an old familiar hotel where he and Henry had stayed. The walls were dull yellow stucco with thick textured paint and dim orange window shutters. He booked three nights in advance, dropped his satchel in the room and walked to the cantina below the hotel.

He sat at the edge of the bar so he could look out the open windows onto the street. There were no other customers in the bar. A dark-haired woman poured him a glass of clear tequila. She sat it beside the bottle of Mexican beer. Through the open windows, he watched the streets become dark with shadow and felt the damp humidity like a wool sweater against his skin. He leaned his forearms against the light wood bar and slouched over his tequila and beer.

The storm came and went. The cloud shadows moved along down the street. A thicker humidity settled down into the bar.

Night came. Neon lights burned all down the road. In the dusk light, when the neon lights and car headlights wrestled with sunlight for dominance, Frank shuffled down the road and got a lay of the land. It had not changed as much as he had thought it might.

He found another cantina further along and drank there, deep into the night. At this bar, the window shutters were closed. An old man played a nylon string guitar while a young dark-haired girl danced. Frank drank mezcal and cold Mexican beers until the bar closed.

***

He made his way down the road and up the steps to his hotel room.

His hands shook, and it was difficult to place the key in the keyhole. He realized he had forgotten to eat. He would have to remember tomorrow. His hands shook the way that Buffalo had shook; she was always leading the way.

The next three days passed in much the same way. The only difference was the weather, and that Frank stayed hidden in shadow until the cool night came.

Antenna Revisited

Looking out through the rain-covered windshield, his hands shaking, Frank steered the LeSabre away from the chipped curb in front of his yellow stucco hotel and began driving out of town, back to the antenna in the cool, rain-damp morning. He remembered every turn. Leaving Ciudad Juárez behind him, the open desert replaced buildings. The landscape was so open there was no place to hide from rain.

He steered off the road into the gravel drive and parked the LeSabre between the radio station—surrounded by rusted chain link fencing—and the towering antenna. He took a deep breath when the LeSabre's engine stopped. Thunder sounded far-off. So far away Frank couldn't see the lightning. The rain had slowed to a drizzle. He stayed in the LeSabre and looked out through the rain-streaked windshield. Dark bunches of weeds reached up around the antenna.

He got out, walked to the end of the gravel lot and kept going, the sound of wet sand crunching under his feet.

The weeds around the antenna bore thorns, and they tore at his suit, into his arms and legs. The weeds reached his chest.

He waded through thorns and weeds all the way to the edge of the antenna. He held his hand out and felt the antenna's rough rusted texture. Its beams were rust colored.

It smelled of iron. Blood. He looked back at where he and Lucinda had laid in the sun. He saw her ghost, laying there, waiting for the shadow of the antenna to pass over her as the day wore on. She didn't say anything. She only smiled and felt the sunlight. He looked away, back up to the sky, to the place where the antenna met the sky. Glancing back, Lucinda was gone. It was all weeds, thorns, cacti, dust.

The clouds were so dark that it almost looked like night, even though the morning should have been getting brighter, edging toward noon. The rain fell harder. Frank could hear raindrops smacking against the ground out in the distance, loud, like an engine with no muffler. Rain pelted into his shoulders, back, arms, and face. His shoes took on water until they felt heavy and loose. The rain felt cold. And it struck so hard that he felt like it would leave red welts on his face and body.

Frank stood for a long time. He looked back to his LeSabre, half a football field behind him, at the edge of the gravel lot, under the dark sky. It didn't look as dull gray in the dark light and rain. He could see himself and Henry standing beside the LeSabre in the cool afterglow of sundown, passing a bottle, seeing their bright future standing out in front of them—reaching into the sky so far they lost sight.

And he saw Henry there in the rain, except he was the same age as he was back then, and he had that same look of fear. That same look he'd had the first time they came here. Frank knew what he was afraid of. He knew then. But he felt it now. There was prophecy in Henry's fear. Knowledge.

The rain went on, and Frank stood until he couldn't

stand any more. And he let himself settle down onto the desert floor, holding onto the leg of the antenna as he descended. And he just sat there, leaning his right shoulder and arm against the antenna's leg, and staring off into the distance—away from the LeSabre, away from the old, brick one-story radio station with its sad, rusted chain-link fence, away from Lucinda's ghost laying in the sunlight of the past, away from Henry's ghost looking out in prophecy over their lives.

Frank leaned against the antenna leg looking out into the distance until his shaking hands slowed, and the rain became gentle, and he fell asleep. He breathed in the blood scent of rust and the smell of the damp, desert rain rising and carrying the scent of wet dirt with it.

Waking up in the middle of the night, Frank found the sky had cleared. He laid on his back under the antenna and looked up at the stars. Orion's bow was just to the left of the antenna. He stared until sleep came again.

The next morning it rained again. A gentle rain. And it kept on for the next two days. Frank stayed under the antenna, standing for hours, sitting, then sleeping. One night he woke up near dawn and slept a while in the car's backseat.

On the morning of the fourth day, he woke up under the antenna, and the sunlight was illuminating his right hand and gray-suit-coated arm. His hands had stopped shaking, and the ghosts of Lucinda and Henry could not haunt him in the daylight even though he was too afraid to look back in their direction. Staring at his feet, he walked through the scrub brush, hearing the thorns tear at his gray suit pants and coat, until he reached the gravel lot.

The Voice of Blood

The scent of blood—that iron smell of rust—was still on Frank's hands, and he smelled it every time he took a draw from his Camel. It was good for the ghost of cigarette smoke to be palpable again. Flesh and blood.

There were four beers left in the sweating ice bucket sitting on the black iron table between Frank and Henry. Drops of water ran down the side of the steel bucket and jumped off like parachuters down through the holes in the iron table to the wood planks of the deck. Frank was glad that the planks were not cedar. And that there was no scent of cedar.

The beer bottle was cold against his leg, and his slacks were damp where it rested. The smell of the burning cigarette took him back. Henry's back was to the honeysuckle-laced fence and the tree line beyond. But there were no pines. And no scent of pine.

Henry's beer bottle rested on the iron table. And the wind clanged the wind chimes hanging from an apple tree in Henry's yard.

"So, what now? You sure you won't stay with us a few days?" Henry looked at Frank and could see the experience of his last year. The wind was cooler in middle America than where Frank had been. He remembered waking up in the night under the antenna, damp with rain, and walking up to sleep in the back seat of the car. And waking up in the car, humid and wanting the movement of air, walking back down to the antenna and laying down again. He never stayed asleep long. It was always waking, sleeping, sitting or standing while leaning against the antenna leg, or lying down in the desert sand—among the scrub brush and lizards. And where did the lizards go when it rained? Underground?

"No, thank you though. Some other time I'll stay. I'm headed back up north. I got a nice place up there. A cabin in Ontario. I got a cat there. Smartest cat you ever saw. Named Buffalo. Best friend I ever had. Neighbor is looking after her." Frank remembered he had a beer bottle in his hand and took a long drink. His cigarette was almost gone. "Gotta get back to her soon. She's waiting." Frank took another draw from his Camel and dropped it into the empty bottle sitting on the iron table.

"Okay," Henry said. "If you're sure you have to go."

"You see the car?" Frank motioned over his shoulder, toward the street.

"That's not the same one, is it?" Henry's beer bottle sat, nearly full, on the iron tabletop between them.

"No." Frank fished a fresh beer out of the ice bucket, twisted its cap off and took a drink. "I tell myself it is, but it isn't. Wonder what became of that old car? I hope somebody drove it in a lake and all its ghosts went underwater and stayed there."

Henry laughed. "Well, that's one way to put it."

"Only way," Frank said. "Don't look back."

"And that's how you live?"

"No, brother. I'm a pillar of salt. Always." The chimes clanged. Frank was glad his suit was dry. He'd gotten it dry cleaned after he left Mexico.

The beers they drank became empty. Frank was ahead of Henry by at least a couple. They took the last two beers out of the steel ice bucket. The late afternoon sunlight was streaming down at an angle from the back of the yard. Frank squinted and the warmth of sunlight made him feel good. But the sunset wasn't far off.

Frank knew he had to leave before sunset came. Before magic time. The edge of things was too pregnant with memories; he was afraid that it would overwhelm him, especially here with Henry.

Frank asked his brother about his life now. He listened. And imagined this foreign life that Henry lived. He paced his beer so that he would stay as long as possible before the soft gold light of dusk fell. The gold light was close now. Frank drank off his last beer.

"Alright, brother, I have to go now." Frank stood up.

"Will you write? Can we visit you there?" It was hard for Frank to live in this moment. He did not want to cry. He did not want to break down. And he could barely stop himself.

Frank nodded. "I'll write if I'm able."

The LeSabre's engine darted to life. The heavy soft light from the setting sun brushed against the right side of the windshield and streamed across the dashboard.

Pulling away from the curb, Frank tried not to think. And tried not to feel.

He took the steel flask from his glove box and took a long drink.

The City of Mother Mary

For the last several weeks, Frank had been living in a motel room with cigarette-burned carpet in the City of Mother Mary. On the Ontario side. The motel was near the dirty river that he had rowed across three times. Each trip had been more vacant. He could not even look at the river anymore.

Light sawed into the room between the edges of the cheap blinds. Judging by the light, Frank guessed it was after one in the afternoon. It was cold now—the combination of further north and time passing. One pitiful dogwood with only a few leaves left stood by the motel parking lot. It was almost winter.

Frank had sold the LeSabre for a loss before he crossed the river. But he did not care. He guessed the money he had would carry him through to the beginning of winter.

During the day, Frank did not leave the room. He would drink Ancient Age bourbon and blackberry brandy, sitting at the edge of the bed in the motel room with wood panel walls. With the TV flashing its light out into his world. He'd buy his bourbon and brandy at the liquor store across the road from the motel.

At night he would walk down to a dimly lit bar that had

sandwiches and beer. He would talk when he had to. He'd order a beer, a sandwich.

The TV light would replace the dim neon reds and blues of the bar; and the bright daylight—devouring the edges of the cheap motel room blinds—replaced the flashing white, reds, and blues from the television.

December

By late December Frank's money was almost gone.
It had gotten cold in the city of Mother Mary.

One morning, Frank woke up in the harsh daylight that spilled like blood into the cracks of his dismal motel room. He put on the tarnished gray suit. Sitting on the edge of the bed, he laced up his black dress shoes, with trembling hands.

He checked out of the motel.

Shivering and shaking, hands pocketed, Frank made his way down the sidewalks of Sault Ste. Marie, Ontario, until he reached the bus stop.

He took the bus as far as it would take him north of town.

He hitched the rest of the way.

When the sun was falling at the edge of the world, Frank reached the woods around Searchmont. He recognized the trailhead of his old path.

Wearing only his gray suit coat and slacks, he walked down the moss-covered path. It was bitterly cold, and Frank could not stop shaking. With every breath the frigid air scraped at his lungs like a razor.

He walked a long time. He was shaking so much that he was nearly not shaking.

The sun had set. For a while, it had broken through at the edge of the old forest. It was getting hard to see the path in front of him. Before it got completely dark, he noticed the turnoff. A narrow trace.

Frank hiked up the trace until he reached the grove of pines that he knew well. He heard spring water gurgling up from the ground. It was a smaller sound now.

Frank's eyes fell on the familiar pine with the smooth gray stone lying beneath it. The place where he had almost died. The place where Buffalo was resting.

When he laid down under the pine, he could smell the pine needle scent. The pine needle bed was soft and warm against his back.

Looking up through the pine branches, he saw a patch of sky caught between day and night. There was no moonlight or stars—only a cloud smear and a haze of afterlight that was hardly there at all.

He wasn't shaking anymore. He closed his eyes and felt the soft pine needle bed beneath him and breathed in the scent of fresh fallen pine needles. He felt warm now.

He was gripped with a feeling of peace. His worry left his mind and the places in his body where it hid. Even though his eyes were closed, he imagined he was still looking up at the sky through the pine branch frame.

He imagined that Orion's bright bow was drawn above him. Against a dark faraway sky that did not frighten him. He was seeing Orion's stars through the skylight in the cabin, and Buffalo was snoring beside him. He was seeing the stars from under the antenna, only Lucinda's ghost had come to life and was laying with him, looking up, and the warm sunlight was on them both, even though it was night. He was seeing the stars from a summer lawn in Mississippi, twisting a fresh grass blade between his thumb and forefinger, and his mom was inside, calling him for lunch.

He was seeing the star of Orion's bow through the windshield of a shining black Buick LeSabre after a long stretch of revivals. He was very tired.

About Etchings Press

Etchings Press is a student-run publisher at the University of Indianapolis that runs a post-publication award—the Whirling Prize—as well as an annual publication contest for one poetry chapbook, one prose chapbook, and one novella. On occasion, Etchings Press publishes new chapbooks from previous winners. For more information about these contests and the Whirling Prize post-publication award, please visit us online at etchings.uindy.edu.

Poetry
2024: *Elliott* by Brian Muriel
2023: *Other Side of Sea* by Xiaoqiu Qiu
2022: *A Place That Knows You* by Tiwaladeoluwa Adekunle
2022: *The Vaudeville Horse* by Elizabeth Kerlikowske
2021: *My Mother's Ghost Scrubs the Floor at 2 a.m.* by Robert Okaji
2020: *Vaginas Need Air* by Tori Grant Welhouse
2019: *As Lovers Always Do* by Marne Wilson
2018: *In the Herald of Improbable Misfortunes* by Robert Campbell
2017: *Uncle Harold's Maxwell House Haggadah* by Danny Caine
2016: *Some Animals* by Kelli Allen
2015: *Velocity of Slugs* by Joey Connelly
2014: *Action at a Distance* by Christopher Petruccelli

Prose
2024: *We Obedient Children* by Karris Rae (fiction and nonfiction hybrid)
2023: *Leaving the House Unlocked* by Elizabeth Enochs (nonfiction)
2022: *Triple Point* by Laura Story Johnson (essays)
2021: *Bad Man Love Stories* by Curtis VanDonkelaar (fiction)
2020: *Three in the Morning and You Don't Smoke Anymore*
          by Peter J. Stavros (fiction)
2019: *Dissenting Opinion from the Committee for the Beatitudes*
          by Marc J. Sheehan (fiction)
2018: *The Forsaken* by Chad V. Broughman (fiction)
2017: *Unravelings* by Sarah Cheshire (memoir)

2016: *Pathetic* by Shannon McLeod (essays)
2015: *Ologies* by Chelsea Biondolillo (essays)
2014: *Static: Stories* by Frederick Pelzer (fiction)

Novella
2024: *Pineville Trace* by Wes Blake
2023: *Our Cadaver* by Elizabeth Toman
2022: *Goodbye to the Ocean* by Susan L. Lin
2021: *Miss Alma May Learns to Fight* by Stuart Rose
2020: *Under Black Leaves* by Doug Ramspeck
2019: *Savonne, Not Vonny* by Robin Lee Lovelace
2018: *Edge of the Known Bus Line* by James R. Gapinski
2017: *The Denialist's Almanac of American Plague and Pestilence*
        by Christopher Mohar
2016: *Followers* by Adam Fleming Petty

Chapbooks from Previous Winners
2022: *slighted...* by Chad V. Broughman (fiction)
2020: *Fruit Rot* by James R. Gapinski (fiction)
2016: *#LOVESONG* by Chelsea Biondolillo (microessays with photos and found text)

Wes Blake's fiction and essays have appeared in *Louisiana Literature Journal, Blood & Bourbon, Book of Matches, Jelly Bucket, White Wall Review,* and elsewhere. His novel, "Antenna," was a semifinalist for the UNO Press Lab Prize. He holds an MFA from the Bluegrass Writers Studio. He lives in Kentucky.

Printed in the USA
CPSIA information can be obtained
at www.ICGtesting.com
LVHW020153160824
788189LV00011B/196

9 781955 521345